Echo in
the Heart

A NOVEL

* * *

Echo in the Heart

A NOVEL

Daniel Hill Zafren

TIME TREASURES

Published by Time Treasures Books, West Jefferson, North Carolina

ISBN 13: 978-0-9833042-0-3

Printed in the United States of America

Cover and interior design by Susan Newman Design, Inc.

The watercolor painting used on the front cover was done on special request to the very talented South Carolina artist, Anna Barnwell-Williams, as appropriate for the story setting and content. It is used here by permission of the artist.

The poem from which the title was derived, as well as the poems or portions of poems set forth at the end of most of the chapters were taken from *Flowers by the Wayside* (1891).

Earlier compelling books by the author, Daniel Hill Zafren:

In a World We Never Made (2001)
A Door Never Opened (2003)
Shadow Selves (2005)
Network of Death (2006)
Not Lost — Just Not Found (2008)
Restless Beauty (2009)
Glimpses of Forgotten Dreams (2010)

www.timetreasuresbooks.com

A Special Note to the Reader

While not absolutely necessary, since a portion
of this book contains a discussion and analysis
of the author's previous seven books, added
value can be had by reading them first.

THE ECHO IN THE HEART

It is not the poet's song,
*   Bidding hopes wild fancies throng:*
It is not the lute-notes clear
That we love, tho' they are dear;
It is but what they impart,
'Tis the echo in the heart.

We may never understand
All the tender, all the grand,
That the poet feels, but still
Pulses thro' our hearts is a thrill,
Something to the hard unknown
Comes to us and us alone.

Every heart has hoped in vain,
Buried deep some lingering pain,
But the memory is stirred
By some lightly spoken word,
And the sudden teardrops start
At the echo in the heart.

Lewis W. Smith

* * *

One

Regina rocked slowly in the old chair on the porch of the main house. The chair creaked, and it was the only sound in the quiet summer evening. In the mountains, the darkness of the country covers nature's sleep until the animals of the night begin their escapades. The stars are vivid, and the lost and yet to be discovered worlds symbolize each person's past and future.

As people age, it is common practice to look back to early periods in their lives. It is an engaging exercise, an engrossing analysis to fix on a time or an event that can be described as a *turning point* or *launching moment* for the scope and direction of one's life.

The beginning of the precious commodities of her life was an easy find. She closed her eyes and the sensation of holding hands with the two friends she made was so real her fingers tingled even though it was more than forty years ago. The joined voices reciting the oath were still fresh and vibrant in her mind.

"Friends for life," they shouted in unison with hands held tightly. "Friends for all yesterdays and tomorrows."

That evening in 1964 as they sat by the campfire they had built by the lake on the last day of summer camp, each recognized and absorbed the meaning of the event. It was almost as if the strength of their grasping of hands extended to their souls. The range and depth of those words would shield and guide them then and through so much of their future. The significance would reverberate throughout their lives and influence all they touched along the way. Great legacies can be ushered in by simple moments.

From the commencement of the special feature of meaning and happiness in her life, Regina liked to think of it as an echo in her heart. As the significance increased and she grew dependent on that happiness, she would measure it in terms of the musical quality of the sound of the echo. At times, the echo was at a crescendo displaying robust power and at others a pianissimo and barely audible.

It was a gentle moment in time, especially for young girls exploring the scope of their feelings and sharing impressions of people and events. Expressions were uninhibited and they bared intimacies of thoughts and emotions. An early discovery was that all they did was far better done together than alone.

Regina Hellerman, Candice Berkle, and Wendy Lavine, were thirteen that summer when they first met at Camp Melody, a summer music camp for girls in the Berkshires. They were in the same bunk, and from the first day were inseparable. Gifted musicians with bubbly personalities, the bond grew stronger with the mutual love and talent for music and with the sharing of the confidences of the awakening bodies and minds. There was also in common a nearly insatiable love of books and an unbounded joy in reading. Talking about the books was nearly as fulfilling as the music that emanated from the depths of their endeavors. Regina, a violinist; Candy, a cellist; and Wendy, a flutist, making soothing and enchanting sounds to light up their world. Each passing day added to the durability of the edifice of friendship. That unity was chambered in their hearts, and it echoed within.

They spent two more wonderful summers together at the camp. They would take walks through the woods, pick wild flowers, and sit on the dock and dangle their feet in the chilly lake water. Reading aloud a favorite passage from a book that caught their fancy was an enjoyable pastime. The voice and content was a remedy for any agitation or apprehension that lurked in the wings. Every activity fostered meaningful thoughts and memories. Repeated warm hugs reinforced the calm security their presence had for each other. Having a best friend is only overshadowed by having two best friends.

It was during the last summer at the camp when they simultaneously experienced kissing a boy for the first time. Every second Saturday night, senior boys from the boy's camp across the lake came over for a social dance in the hall on the second floor of the boathouse. At that last social for the summer, the strict camp director, who never would have tolerated such behavior, was sick and confined to the infirmary. The rebellious and sympathetic counselors turned off the lights during the last slow dance of the evening, and each of the boys they were dancing with kissed them full on the lips. Wendy was to confess afterwards that the boy who kissed her also stuck his tongue in her mouth. While the thought of it was disgusting, she gushingly described it to her friends as an exciting experience.

They lived in different cities and between the camp sessions there were constant telephone discussions. Talking about music, books, and observations of events and people consumed lengthy telephone time. Any topic, even if explored before, had nearly the same enchantment as Wendy's first French kiss.

Intruding on the sheltered tower of friendship was the growing tension and disruption of a volatile time in the nation's history. The Vietnam War precipitated an already broadening dividing line between the young and the rest of society. Youth movements and protests congealed the need and desire to have a culture of their own. Youngsters were swept along in the swift current and the absorbing charisma of the beatnik generation. The call beckoned for youngsters to join the throng rebelling against societal dictates, parental control, and governmental restraints. The allure of these distractions infringed on their desired evolution. The music of the revolution held them in its grasp between classical undertakings. Between the reading of the classics and other enticing writings, they were immersed in the testaments and thoughts of the radical student leaders. The abandonment of dress codes prevailed, and they wore the garments of protest, outlandish and clashing combinations whether or not attractive in conventional sights. The pleading of parents fell on deaf ears.

Regina, also known to those close to her as Ginny, lived with her parents in New York City. As an only child, her doting parents had bestowed on her all of the distinct advantages of a culturally rich city. Early piano lessons confirmed a love and talent for music, and eventually she became enamored with the violin. Her parents could easily afford the best violin teachers, and at the age of sixteen Regina was admitted to the renowned School for the Performing Arts.

Even during the beatnik period, the parents tolerated Regina's erratic behavior believing the particular person she was would prompt a special individuality after the phase ran its course. As a young girl, the coal dark eyes in an oval face surrounded by long flowing black hair set her apart from most children. The frail beauty emanated from the long slender fingers, fingers designed to make divine music.

Inner conflicts are most difficult to resolve, particularly for young and spirited people. Regina was inwardly torn between wanting to belong and conform to the youth movement and losing herself in her music and books. Helpless in controlling the course of events, she could only hope that the true person she was meant to be would emerge. She had a feeling it would be an agonizing trip. Conflict brings frustration and a gnawing impatience. It seemed as if the only comforting moments came in the telephone connections with Wendy and Candy. Their words expressing similar desires and dilemmas held them in sync.

The friends also shared any intruding unhappiness. Perhaps, it is more important to have people share the down moments as happiness is often its own adhesion. The trying moments can use the comfort and support of a kindred spirit to take the edge off of the demands and conflict. Another aspect of the friendship so valuable to each of them was that they shared the concern for one another. They felt the pangs of any unhappiness and disappointment. An air of caring prevailed in each and every trying moment. All of this was accompanied by an outlook that any adversity would be overcome and obliterated by the prospect and promise of the next life adventure. A line from her readings of the works of Frances Bacon had stayed with her. *A principal fruit of friendship is the ease and discharge of the fullness and swellings of the heart, which passions of all kinds do cause and induce.* The friendship was a primary source of the echo in her heart.

Throughout Regina's high school years, none of the boys at the school captured her interest. Some paid growing attention to her and suggested dating. Her mother urged her to accept such invitations assuring her that only by dating could she know what a person was like and what kind of person she wanted to be with. Regina did not agree with that. She steadfastly believed that by closely observing people in various situations and by talking with them to gauge reactions, such would be the criteria to know whether a person was worth getting close to. The dream of romance lingered in her heart. Music, books, and friendship were sufficient for now.

Candice Berkle was more of a dreamer, more of a blossoming romantic. Everyone called her Candy, and she reserved *Candice* only for formal use. She lived with her parents and two younger brothers in a modest house in Providence, Rhode Island. She was the only one in the family bestowed with musical ability. The other members did not share her interest. Her parents believed a musician lurked deep in the family history, but they were not sure and none of the relatives could pinpoint any confirmation of that fact. When Candy developed a desire to play the cello, little did the family know it would become a driving obsession. Fortunately, the talent matched the earnest drive. There were no formal cello teachers nearby, but a lady, Pauline Hardwine, retired from the Philharmonic Orchestra as a cellist lived some twenty miles away. Upon discovering Candy's gift, she readily agreed to drive to the Berkle home to oversee the development of the budding musician. It was this same lady who suggested Candy go to Camp Melody. All of these lessons and the camp were a financial hardship for the family. Yet, the sweet sounds of Candy's talent convinced them that the sacrifice was necessary. They surely did not understand her wayward form of dressing and talk of youthful rebellion, and the summer's absence was an attractive respite.

Candy's increasing romantic yearnings, fostered by the melodies her instrument made as well as the readings of the great poets and philosophers, transported her to imaginary heights of all the arts. She tried her hand at poetry, painting, and sculpting. She believed the prominent freckles and flaming red hair were a sign of creativity and allure to be greeted and appreciated by a young man similarly endowed who would eventually cross her path and capture her heart. An abiding crush developed for any radical youth leader that came to the forefront.

In the meantime, the richness of the friendship she enjoyed with Regina and Wendy bolstered her morale and esteem. She counted herself fortunate to have such meaningful thoughts and convictions. She could not get that with any of her classmates, and surely it was the substance and expanse of music and the intensity of thoughts and ideas from reading that enriched the closeness. Hearts and minds reveled in the avid devotion to the deep emotions evoked by the great composers and writers. Historical significance bestowed on new blood to catapult souls through the ages.

Each time Wendy Lavine looked at the two-inch scar above her right thumb, she thought of Regina and Candy as the initial pain was severe from the scrape by the rusty nail at the camp. The bleeding and the tetanus shot were still vivid in her mind. Each time she played the flute, the scar faced her and it had become over time not only a symbol of the close friendship but also of her humanity. There were other scars she had to bear. Since her father's untimely death when she was four, it had been stressful living with her mother who could not escape the emotional and financial pain of that premature demise. Uncle Fred, her father's brother, was an interesting and attentive man who lived close by with his family in the same New Jersey town. He included Wendy in his family's life, and even took her with them on their Saturday morning ritual of frequenting as many yard sales as possible. They would swing by and pick Wendy up. On one such occasion a flute was for sale. With fascinating rapture, Wendy picked it up. Uncle Fred noted the sparkle in her eyes and was able to negotiate a low price with the seller. Wendy took it home, cleaned it up, and spent hours experimenting with its sounds and exploring its possibilities. Uncle Fred found some books on learning to play the flute, and Wendy was hooked on the musical magic that set her soul free. Self-taught, the flute became an amazing living object in her hands. She had an uncanny ear for music and could replicate melodies she heard only once. The only thing she dreamed of was to play the flute in a famous orchestra, later imagining Ginny and Candy there as well.

Wendy's mother neither recognized nor appreciated the youngster's talent, but Uncle Fred sensed the presence of musical genius housed in that petite frame. It was Uncle Fred who financed Wendy's tuition at the music camp, and he just knew his deceased brother would have thanked him for giving the child a chance to blossom. The gift of a professional flute sealed the progress with promise.

Wendy had straight brown hair, and her features were rather plain. Yet, her personality rose to the level of her music and she was unrestrainable in speaking her mind much to the shock and often secret admiration of others. As a self-taught musician and a self-made person there would be no denying her dreams. She could not afford to buy books and was a frequent visitor to the library that was a short walk from her home. The support and mingling of intellectual involvement by Regina and Candy was her castle in the sky.

The three young ladies believed their destiny was as one. There was no way they would risk a future together. As they entered the senior year in their separate high schools, plans were made to go to the same college. The basic requirements were that the college had to have a separate school of music, a full orchestra, and music scholarships readily available. It would be all or nothing, and nothing was not an option.

And many a lesson of life I heed
  On the beautiful ivy clad wall —
Twere better to climb over rough rocks I read
  Than never to climb up at all!

And I learn again from the bird in the gleams.
  That joy will most surely abide
With those who dwell longest on pleasure-fraught dreams,
  Who look most on life's sunny side.

The Joy,
W. Eddy

Echo in the Heart

* * *

Two

Appalachian State University, also know by its initials ASU and the shortened App. State, is a coed liberal arts college in the Blue Ridge Mountains of North Carolina. It quickly became the main focus of attention. It had a separate Music School with an eminent musical faculty, an orchestra with an outstanding reputation, and it offered a number of music scholarships.

Regina was the first to receive a full scholarship. The well-known violin teachers eased the way for her. Mrs. Hardwine was able to assist Candice in obtaining a scholarship. Her contacts in the world of music from the many years playing with the Philharmonic enabled Candy's application to bypass any potential obstacles. Wendy, fortunately, did get a tryout mainly because of the high praise coming from Regina and Candy. That was all a super talent needs. The music panel was enthralled by her performance and unanimously voted to have a full scholarship extended to her. At times, even fate needs a helping hand.

The college, located in the quaint town of Boone, is also surrounded by an assortment of ski resorts and other country inns. Freshmen were required to be in a dormitory, but due to the mushrooming enrollment there were not enough dormitory rooms to house the incoming class. An exception from dormitory residence was extended to students on a scholarship, presumably because they would be able to pay for private facilities since they did not have to pay tuition and because the need to maintain the scholarships would not be put at risk by any unacceptable behavior.

Even though the Vietnam War was over and the beatnik environment waning, there was still a proliferation of radical thought and behavior on college campuses. ASU was no different. Clashing attire appeared throughout the student body, and the loudest voices in opposition to authority came from chosen and admired leaders. The culturally diverse students, as a reservoir, sloshed in every direction and often spilled out beyond its confined limits. A restless spirit prevailed, and good intentions were often gobbled up in a frenzy of wasted energy. The beliefs of yesterday tormented the explorers of new adventures and the fog hanging over the future provided a backdrop of uncertainty and frustration.

The girls found a loft apartment above a stationery store, and it seemed like the perfect place. It did not have separate bedrooms, but the closeness was not a distraction for kindred hearts and spirit. It had a large living space to spread out things important to their existence. At the times when the store would be closed, the music would not bother anyone.

The apartment was partially furnished, mainly with adequate beds for the three of them and a complete kitchen. They found a consignment shop where they picked up an assortment of decorating items to match their independence and rambling dreams. Little matched and they could not care about decorating style. An interior decorator would undoubtedly shriek upon spying on the purposeful unsanctioned contents of what is supposed to be living quarters. For the inhabitants, as long as their personalities congealed and their music harmonized, everything else was secondary.

In their quest for maturity and thirst for independence, music was the intimate communication between their souls. At other times, without prediction or hesitation, lengthy philosophical discussions on the meaning of life and their developing beliefs spilled forth. Many of the theories were formulated by writings of the giant philosophers of the past, the supreme thinkers. These sessions were usually uplifting but at other times troubling. Their probing minds and the freedom to delve into forbidden subjects comforted them, but the realization of how little they really knew about applying ideas to life situations was very unsettling. They discussed many a time the concept by a host of philosophers that a person is such a variable creature and so strong-willed and individualistic that one must learn, if at all, from one's own experience alone. Limited experience does stultify the desire for broadening horizons. They likened themselves to the *Bloomsbury Group*, which had been made up of British intellectuals, such as Virginia Woolf, with a passion for books and a desire to become creative readers.

One early conversation was especially memorable, and in later years they would recall, rehash, and embellish on what was said. It was a Saturday night, a prominent dating night. None of them had dated since arrival at the college, and not a single male had shown any interest in the trio. They had gotten into their pajamas early, made popcorn and munched on it as they sat on the carpet by the sofa.

Wendy, in her usual unabashed manner, was the first to speak. "Here we have it, folks, the musical version of the ugly duckling."

The two other girls chuckled. Candy was quick to respond. "Don't you mean ducklings, or is the plural duckli?"

Regina chimed in, "All you need is one to serve as a symbol. None of us should feel ugly. We are just undiscovered. What is beauty, anyway? It is merely a mirage, a fleeting adornment that cannot hold a candle to talent, integrity, expanse of personality, and depth of feelings. And, dear sisters of my heart, we have all of that and more."

"If you say so," Candy interjected. "I'm not going to argue with you. In fact, I'm all for appointing you as our spokesman."

"The successful formula," Wendy began in a hushed voice, "Is to make sure others are of the same opinion. Notably, I might add, some fellow of equal, or if even possible of higher character and stature, to sweep us off our feet."

"While you two have been totally absorbed in orchestral and academic functions," Candy offered in dramatic fashion, "I have been closely examining the boys in the orchestra. After all, music is not only a lifeline, it is an emotional and intellectual attachment. A man of music is prime material for any romantic involvement since there is already a common thread of sensitivity. Several of them are likely candidates for worship by ugly duckli. We have already thrown social proprieties away, so maybe we should turn aggressive. With each passing day, I believe more that life does not come to us. We need to go and find it."

"Without a road map or guide book?" Wendy feigned surprise.

"Precisely," Candy continued, "If we use existing references then it is not our personal quest. We are just following someone else's plan, walking in someone else's footsteps. We need really to break new ground, and make a path where none now exists."

"Tempting, but dangerous," Regina announced.

"Not to mention," Wendy frowned, "How can there be any males with higher qualities than possessed by the dream sisters?"

Regina quickly picked up on this thread of thought. "Now that is the promise. Not to live it but to dream it. Anything is possible in dreams."

"Why only in dreams?" Candy stood up and stretched. "If you can dream it, you can live it. I firmly believe that."

Regina stood as well. "Speaking about dreams, what I have always wondered about is why I am in all of my dreams. I suppose I am the only one living them, but if I can think of situations in which I am not involved why is the dream always revolving around me. It starts with me, and if I dream it through it ends with me."

Standing to join the others, Wendy chimed in," My dreams are not vivid and they are rather disjointed, even if I remember them or parts of them. I usually wake up, and if I fall back to sleep the dream has already gone the way of a note I have played and cannot capture."

Before falling asleep that night, and on nights yet to come, they would each think about the process of dreaming and the substance of dreams. After all, a dream is as personal as anything might be. It is yours alone, and perhaps no description can do it full justice. It is like that old riddle: What is completely yours but is used more by others than yourself? It is your name.

The next day, Candy had retrieved a poem she had remembered by Edgar Allan Poe that professes that all we see or seem to be is but a dream within a dream.

Take this kiss upon thy brow!
And, in parting from you now
This much let me avow—
You are not wrong, to deem
That my days have been a dream;
Yet if Hope has flown away
In a night or in a day
In a vision, or in none,
Is it there for the less gone?
All that we see or seem
Is but a dream within a dream.

Regina was surprised she remembered as much detail of the discussion as she did. Yet, there were so many moments of the past that clearly stood out in her memory, a testament to moments to cherish. That discussion seemingly barely covering the surface of a subject represented not so much a probing intellect than the limitless containment of thought and conversation. It engendered a type of freedom blending mind and spirit that had no confines. A discussion between them would be as a talk one might have alone. There were no barriers, no censorship, and no artificial expectations. It was the nucleus of the primary composition of their essence. All later discussions, be they short or long, would be additional steppingstones on their pathway through life. Another sort of dream, no doubt.

Our yesterdays! A dream! They sped so fast
     We scarce could think what priceless blessings came
To gladden them, till all their hours were passed,
     And only memory brought them back again.

Life's Yesterdays
D. E. Millard

Echo in the Heart

* * *

Three

Ah, the allure and mystery of romantic relationships! Poets believe it is a matter of destiny. Others know it is more just a case of physical attraction and emotional interest that arises when, coincidentally, paths cross. Yet, each story has a captivating uniqueness even if just for the telling that is carried forth in poignant memories. Each is a catalyst prompting a desire for recognition and acknowledgement.

The sound of the screen door opening snapped Regina back from her distant thoughts. Candy and Wendy came out from the house and sat in adjoining rocking chairs. Being together for more than forty years, words were unnecessary to affirm the security and pleasure of being at each other's side. They rocked gently in unison, enjoying the coolness of the mountain air on a summer's night.

A light came on down in the barn, and they knew their husbands were getting the produce ready and loaded to sell the following morning at the Farmer's Market in West Jefferson. It was done with little fanfare, unlike earlier days when all of the children were still here and would revel in making a commotion of even the steadfast of actions. The fullness of life is measured by past contentment, present satisfaction, and a gentle future prospect.

"I was just thinking of how we met our love slaves," Regina spoke nearly in a whisper.

"Correction," Candy was quick to say in a hushed tone, "How I was instrumental, excuse the pun, in conquering the male-dominated world. How quickly they forget the unsung, excuse the pun, heroes."

At that time, little did the three young men in the orchestra suspect that they were to be themselves the orchestrated score of enchantment. The further fact that the three were also registered in the same English class as the ladies on The Great Books indicated the mutual action of reading and its appreciation in the scheme of growing up.

One of the men had already gained a form of notoriety apart and distinct from his clarinet playing. Archer Menton was also the President of the Students for Democratic Action, the most vocal and active radical group on the campus. Coming from a Quaker family such was a dramatic change of ideas and behavior

15

for him. The romantic inclination of Candy's attention to radical leaders made it a natural connection. The poor fellow did not stand a chance of avoiding her charm and beguiling way, and the two quickly became a couple.

Candy could easily recall the first date she had with Archer. He freely espoused noble causes, and his dramatic anger towards society's intractability as well as his belief in the power of the individual was enthralling to her. More than once he uttered his favorite line by W. K. Clifford: *[I]t is wrong always, everywhere, and for anyone, to believe anything upon insufficient evidence.* He was quick to boast that his rightful place in history was there at Appalachian State. "Most people think the sit-in as a form of demonstration against authority started with the Civil Rights Movement. Wrong. It started right her at App. State. In the 30s, the then Chancellor was extremely strict about fraternization. Boys and girls could not socialize and he even had them sit on opposite sides of the court at basketball games. At just one of these games, the boys and girls sat together and refused to budge no matter how much he ranted and raved. He expelled them all, but that did not change the fact that the sit-in was born."

Archer had his own demons to do battle with. His Quaker background was a blessing, but it also held him back from putting his entire energy in anything he believed in. Causes were tempered by the serenity of his upbringing. Music and the constant awakening of the love of reading were the only features of his existence that he could become totally immersed in. Classical music records playing were the background to his infancy and young years. Both of his parents dabbled in music, but the soothing tones playing almost constantly in the home were the foundation of their religious faith. His father played the clarinet now and then, and it seemed natural for him to show his son the instrument and teach him what he knew about it. Archer took it from there. The clarinet became an additional appendage, and accompanied by a keen ear for music and the classical favorites so much a part of his environment took on a new life through his emulation. A family friend taught him to read music, and that key unlocked limitless possibilities for an undaunted talent.

Music had its major role in the love that grew with Candy. Together, meaningful moments became a life symphony. His ideas accompanied by her animation, constructed on a foundation of an absorption of music and with the ideals espoused by the philosophers of yesteryear, and the love was no less than right.

Archer introduced his roommate, Freeman Carpenter, to Wendy, and it did not take long for those two to realize they were a perfect match. Freeman played the French horn in the orchestra and came from a line of generations that played that very instrument. Even though relatively inexperienced in matters involving the opposite sex, it did not take him long to know that being paired with Wendy, Freeman was no longer a free man. Each time that he would peer into those dazzling gray eyes and feel that gentle touch on his arm, it was as if a life companionship was self-defined. His parents, once thinking that his quiet nature might be indicative of homosexual tendencies, were grateful that he had taken up with a female musician, and they turned their attention to two younger siblings who were constantly getting in trouble with school authorities. Those two had no interest or talent in the realm of music. Many a time the parents were puzzled by the radically different result from a similar upbringing. A common mystery, perhaps, in many families.

It was John Bingham who pursued Regina. Being the violinist sitting to her left, the perfect profile was the first feature that caught his attention. The concentration and determination to conquer the music were traits that solidified this interest. After some passing remarks led to extended conversations, he then became enamored by her smile and easy laughter. Their first date confirmed his resolve to make this the love of his life, and that in turn ignited a fervent attraction to him. A warm and comfortable aura led to her now famous statement on the following day after orchestra practice, a statement that would become a legend for the players in succeeding years. Pointing to her violin bow, she said in dramatic fashion, "This is my bow," followed by a nod in John's direction, "And this is my other beau."

Regina had fallen in love with John not because of her romantic inclination. It was the culmination of the deep-set values that a close friendship had ignited. A mate is the extension of a friendship, a person who is also there for you and you for him. Within the concept of best friends is an expanding universe to enfold more than one person and capable of accommodating multiple capacities.

"So, here we are," Wendy began in a hushed voice. "Another special night because we are together to enjoy it. We could easily be back at Camp Melody. So much has happened, yet nothing has really changed at all."

"I look at my hands, farmer's hands, that keeps me from bringing my cello to full life," Candy sighed, "And I know how much has changed. I know you are referring to a full heart which has given us a rich life, but at times if I close my eyes really tight I can see me in a dream bowing to a delirious audience at Carnegie Hall."

Regina smiled. "Music is still a vital part of our being. Don't we play all together nearly every day? And, the children, all gifted so that when they come to visit a family recital is inevitable just as we had such sessions when they were growing up. Carnegie Hall cannot replace that kind of performance. And the love of books we instilled in them surely becomes a masterpiece of its own. We need to take great pride overall that we have done well with our lives. Our dreams are living things, leading us to where we want to be."

"Do you think any of the children will return here to the farm to live the kind of life we chose?" Wendy's voice trailed off as if she already knew they were out there now living lives of a different kind but also of their own choice.

Each rose slowly thinking back in unison. The three couples bound by love and music had finished their years at Appalachian State. Instead of pursuing careers in music, what appealed to them the most was communal living. It was a banner of the time and a message of hope for the future. They had studied the concept and visited a number of the famous and successful communes already started. The one feature that they did not agree with and which prevented them from joining an existing commune was the freedom of lovemaking. Call them old-fashioned in this regard, but they felt strongly in the sanctity of marriage. So, they knew they had to have their own commune. They married in a triple civil ceremony, parents and relatives shaking their heads in disbelief but having to accept what was believed to be inevitable since it was explained over and over again that such was the way it was going to be.

Still enchanted by the North Carolina mountains, they borrowed money wherever they could to put a down payment on a twelve-acre farm with a pond near West Jefferson. They named it *Moon Music Farm* after an old poem that Candy had saved from her readings of poetry when she was trying her hand at it herself.

MOON MUSIC

Blond moonbeams shine in symphonies of light
  Upon the surface of a sleeping lake,
Blue shadows, deep in dormant depths opaque
Flit under dainty ripples, moonlit, bright.

Around the myriad voices of the night
  Blend with the moon's vague song, and make
    Wonderful concerts of soft tunes, that break
In foam, in sheen, in tuneful, soulful flight.

Sound like the kiss of wave upon a pearl —
Sound like the flesh thrill of an amorous girl —
Music so dream like subtle, that no ear
  Save that of muser can enjoy its balm,
Sound like the murmur of a falling tear —
  Sound like a twilight hush of endless calm.

Francis S. Saltus

They grew a variety of vegetables and planted fruit trees in the fertile mountain soil to feed them, selling any surplus at local farmers' markets. They planted as many fruit tress as they could, primarily apple trees, and as the trees matured bountiful harvests greeted them. They then started growing Fraser Firs, as the county was famous for such a specialty Christmas tree shipped all across the nation. Once the trees reached maturity, an infusion of money allowed them to buy an adjoining seventy-one acre parcel to expand their operations to a major commercial enterprise.

The six did not neglect music, and they played together whenever they could as the music supported the lean and trying times and was a form of celebration for the better days. Peaceful moments engendered reading and discussions about the books and the thinkers profusely setting forth opinions. The words of Robert Louis Stevenson had forever opened their eyes. *In noble books we are moved with something like the emotions of life.*

The children were taught and grew to love music, and frequent musical ensembles highlighted the otherwise bountiful endeavors. The children thought of them as jam sessions since bluegrass music was often their choice of refrains. All of the children were home-schooled, and each had in effect six attentive teachers and six loving parents. Books were their truest acquaintances.

Regina and John had Ricky, now thirty-one, and living with his wife Jean, in Atlanta. Ricky met Jean while they were at Appalachian State, and Ricky went on to become a psychoanalyst and Jean a computer specialist.

Wendy and Freeman had Felicia, now twenty-nine and Mandy, now twenty-eight. Both went to Appalachian State, of course, and both now shared a town home in Charlotte. Felicia was a banking broker and Mandy a legal secretary. Both were unmarried, but they led an active social life even though they preferred to go to the farm on as many weekends as they could. Both were adamant in saying they would not marry until they met a man like their father or like Uncle John or Uncle Archer. The close-knit families considered the other parents as uncles and aunts and the other children as siblings. A communal kitchen with an extra large picnic table to accommodate the entire family, and usual after dinner musicals fostered a special type of togetherness.

Candy and Archer had Adam, now thirty-four, and after leaving Appalachian State he became an accountant in Philadelphia. It seemed appropriate to name him Adam since he was the first male baby in the *Moon Music Farm* clan. He had married Helene, a piano teacher, and they had a baby girl, now five years old, aptly named Eve. It was the group's first grandchild and niece, and all doted on her.

The holidays were filled with special appeal as the family gathered at the farm, amply referred to as living *the old times*. Love, music, books, and laughter prevailed, and the dream sisters would sigh often and hug whatever body passed them by. Hearts were overflowing, and each confirmed they had made all of the right life choices. It was a testament to emphasize a remarkable echo in the heart.

As this summer's night wore on, on impulse, they reached across and held hands as they did around the campfire as youngsters. They had no idea that their lives were about to change forever.

Some there are as gay and careless
In their glad prosperity,
As the bright hued wild flowers nodding
On the cliffs above the sea;
For their hearts are filled with pleasures,
And their thoughts are of their own.
So they care not for the struggles,
Griefs, and trials, of those thrown
Like the sea-weeds, by the breakers,
On the rocks each ruined form
Marred and broken — a grim relic
Of life's storm.

A Sea Thought
Helena M. Tucker

Echo in the Heart

* * *

Four

The following morning, a thick fog clung to the valleys and the mountains. The men debated about whether they should leave at the usual early hour to go to the market. Since the truck was fully loaded, and they knew many folks would brave the elements to get there early for the best selections, they decided to leave at the regular time so that they would be fully set up for the crowd of buyers.

It was uncertain how the accident happened. The best that could be reconstructed was that John was driving and the other two men were also on the bench seat next to him, and in the fog John probably lost vision of the road and the truck went down a steep embankment crashing into a tree. Nobody saw the truck for hours until the fog lifted. The three men were dead, and it was thought merciful to put in the police report that the men died instantly even though the police were unsure if one or more may have lived for a brief time.

It was late morning when the state trooper pulled into the farm. The ladies could see the dust from the dirt road of the lane leading to the house, and while it was a bit early for the men to return, if they had sold out there would have been no reason to hang around at the market. Just as the trooper got out of the car, a large dark cloud blocked the sun.

Tragedy can occur anywhere and at any time. It can have massive impact or be limited in effect to just a few people. There is no escaping that its result is final. In shocking disbelief, the three women clutched at each other as tears flowed unabated. They held on to one another long into the night. After the children were called, they held on to one another as the only rational action. The night silence was only broken by an occasional sob. If the telephone did ring, it remained unanswered. While difficult at earlier times, it probably was fortuitous that none of the men's parents were still alive.

The men were buried with just the family present near the large weeping willow tree by the pond. Many a picnic was held under that tree and the men especially enjoyed the picnics. Archer had even remarked once that the tree seemed to have musical qualities the way the boughs dangled like a note yet to be played.

The next day, their friend Pastor Tom Vestal graciously offered and held a

23

memorial service at the Mission Home Baptist Church. Although not churchgoers, Pastor Tom was fond of the family and he knew that religion is in the heart and mind and not necessarily on a bench in a church.

The crowd overflowed into the parking lot. For the many years that the families had been there, they had made many friends at the farmer's market and through the music they played at or sponsored by the Ashe County Arts Council. Each had also volunteered at a host of local functions and at civic organizations. Many wanted to offer words of remembrance, but it was decided that after a blessing by Pastor Tom only the children would speak of their fathers followed by closing words by the wives.

The children discussed what would be said, and they thought it best to talk about one special memory of their fathers. Adam, as the eldest, would speak first. Before speaking, he noted the tears on his mother's face. He had seen tears of joy on Candy's face over the years when she laughed so hard, but these were a different sight. He glanced at his wife, Helene, enfolding their daughter, Eve, in a tight embrace. He cleared his throat. "The meaning of family is better felt than spoken about. As the eldest of the *Moon Music Farm* offspring, I will probably say similar things as my spiritual brother and sisters. We have been luckier than most, having in reality three sets of parents to love us and for us to love. Losing one father is bad enough, but to lose three is a devastating blow to our family." He paused, again seeing the daylight glisten on Candy's tear-streaked cheek. "My dad, Archer Menton, was truly a very special man. His strong belief that the world could and should be a better place was a driving force his entire life. I remember our first serious talk as if it were yesterday. I was eleven, and I had been working by his side in the tree field. He said, 'Let's take a break, son.' He then proceeded to tell me all about his life, his beliefs, how he fell in love with mom, and that they all would be there for me so that I should never feel alone no matter what lay ahead for me. I felt as if he was talking to a grownup. I decided right then and there that I would try not to disappoint him. I hope I never did. Little wonder that my father will always be my hero. The words of Ralph Waldo Emerson as he described Thoreau seem most appropriate to repeat here: *His soul was made for the noblest society; he had in a short life exhausted the capabilities of this world; wherever there is knowledge, wherever there is beauty, he will find a home.*"

"Dear friends and dearest moms, and my very special mother, Wendy

Carpenter. My name is Felicia Carpenter, and I am usually lost in the daily battles of the financial world. I never suspected I would ever have to do something this difficult, to talk about an overwhelming presence in my life cruelly taken away. As Adam said, we are probably the most fortunate and blessed people in the world. As children, and even as adults, we have had the nurturing and love of three mothers and three fathers. Perhaps, only now when half of that powerful combination is physically gone do I fully realize that emotionally that grouping will always be intact. They live on in us, their children. The sounds of their meaningful advice and warm endearments stay with us just as the refrains of their music echo in our hearts. Mandy and I lovingly always called our father *Poppa*. He was a shining light that guided and protected us through the growing years and well beyond. His ardent and gentle love for our mom," she paused long enough to blow a kiss to Wendy who sobbed quietly holding the hands of Regina and Candy on either side of her, "Was and is a standard that may prove difficult for us to ever find suitable husbands. But, we will settle for no less. When I was twelve, *Poppa* and I went fishing, as we often did, at the old pond. Mandy hated the worms, so she usually stayed behind. It gave me some precious moments with the man who to me is larger than life. On this one time, he suggested we forego the fishing and we lay down on the soft ground under the imposing weeping willow tree by the pond. Lying on our backs side-by-side, he reached for my hand and his gentle musician hands conveyed what words cannot at times adequately express. As always, he encouraged me to speak my mind, and I opened up to him about my growing inner fear of ever leaving the security of *Moon Music Farm* and having to face a harsh and what I believed would be an unforgiving world. He told me that he had felt such doubts about an unrelenting world at one point in his youth, but he would watch the birds in his yard and would imagine that he had wings so he could fly. He recited the old saying that the two best things a parent can give to a child are roots and wings. He carefully explained that I had wings if I just imagined them, powerful wings to carry me to any destination and to bring me back home if any outside place proved uninviting or unwanted. I have lived by that image ever since. I can go or do whatever I want, and yet know that I can always return to the nest. This provides great inner strength. So, *Poppa*, while I will miss you terribly, as the song lyrics aptly describe, you are the wind beneath my wings."

Her steps were slow and tentative as she walked to the front of the gathering. "I am Mandy Carpenter. As you can plainly see, I am the smallest and the frailest of the *Moon Music Farm* brood. I never demanded more love because of my stature, but it always seemed that the adults as well as my sister and brothers bestowed it on me. Having such an expansive family has taught me that there are no limitations on love, and if we all had the notion to do it we could love everyone in the world. It was not easy for me to grow up on a farm. I could not do strenuous chores and I was squeamish about all of the natural components of country life. *Poppa* turned it all into a game. Knowing I loved puzzles and riddles, he would relate all I saw and touched as parts of real life that my imagination could reject or could try to solve or fit together as a composite picture. I cannot select any special one memory of him. It is all enduring and loving of him as a person and as my *Poppa*." She cried uncontrollably, and there was not a dry eye in the church.

Ricky Bingham kissed his wife, Jean, before moving to the front of the assemblage. He cleared his throat and fixed his gaze on Regina, his mother. Such a sad face on one of the happiest people he had ever known. "My sisters and brother have proven once again that eloquence comes from the heart. We are separate persons and yet are one. Our relationship and our meaningful upbringing with all of our parents give full significance to family. It is a unity that defies weakening or diminishing even in the face of a monumental and tragic loss. Our family embrace enfolds all of you who have come today, all whose lives our family has touched. Sharing this grief is a tribute to our fathers. Thank you. My mothers will speak shortly and thank you as well. One special mother, Regina, my birth mother, is the symbol of all we are. Imagine, if you will, a small boy, entranced by his mother and father playing a duet on their violins. The instruments were alive, and after they taught me to play and encouraged me to join them in the music, I felt I had reached a high plateau in the scheme of life. Even now, when I play the violin it brings me ever so close to the love they shared and bestowed on my siblings and me. It accentuates the truism that it is not the years in your life that are important but the life in your years. My dad, John Bingham, continues to live on in us, continues to inspire and perpetuate the love I have for my wife, Jean. My dad showed me by example that to be loved is good but the greatest attribute is to love another. When I say by example, the way he would reach for mom's hand, stroke her arm, and accompany her in so many common endeavors. The way he would wink at me when he thought his added attention made her happy. When I was very young, he would wait until mom finished reading me a story at bedtime and then tuck me in, and then he would sneak in for a kiss on the forehead. Once he explained the ritual by saying the kiss was a way of letting my body know there was a connection, an indestructible connection, with my parents. The kiss would always be there even if my mother and father were not there to replant it. It was a way of knowing that I was never alone. His life has been tragically cut short. Yet, his accomplishments fill many lifetimes. Dad, you will always be loved."

The service had already been emotionally draining, and the wives had yet to show the contents of their hearts. Wendy was the first to speak, clutching a handful of tissues already wet from continuous tears. In a choked voice, with every ear in the church bent toward the speaker, she began while directly looking at her sisters of the heart. "Freeman was the center of my world, the only man I ever loved and ever could love. In all of the years being together, I found no fault in him. There were just ever-increasing reasons to love him. I will never stop loving him. Thank you for being here as a tribute to his life". Felicia rushed to the front to help her back to her seat. Not a weak woman, the wear of the deaths, the burial, and now this gathering, it was apparent she was physically and emotionally exhausted.

Candy clasped Wendy's hand when she sat down and walked slowly to the front. "As an emotional outlet when I was young, I wrote poetry. Last night, to calm my unsettled spirit, I wrote this poem for my beloved Archer. Please bear with me.

>As a brook winding through the meadow
>>I know I must and will go on as I grow old;
>Not as the person I was but as a mere shadow
>>Since the water has tuned dark and cold.
>
>I shall hold and kiss him in the flesh no more,
>Yet, I will embrace his memory evermore."

Regina kissed Candy's cheek and she rose to make her way to the front. "As I listened to all of my family with their loving thoughts, I know we have all had more from life than most people ever experience. The loss of my soul mate and my two brothers does not detract from that. Rather, it accentuates it. I will always be grateful for the time I had with him and always feel deprived that it was not longer. He carried my love for him when he was buried, and I wear his love for me wrapped around me for all I will be and do. We love you all for sharing these memories. The three men are true examples of the best that humanity has to offer."

Afterwards, folks dropped in at the farm to gather for a last farewell and to support the family. Helene and Jean had made a large pot of chili the night before, and Pastor Tom had brought loaves of fresh bread that his wife, Martha, made from scratch and was well known for by many in the area. Others brought dishes of food. Piercing the silence of the absence of the men was the sharing of grief, a very potent weapon to dull the impact of loss.

The next day, the children left. Hugs and tears traveled with them as they tried to resume lives with the determination the fathers would have wished for. Alone, the three women sat on the rockers holding hands. Yesterdays were gone, and tomorrows uncertain. Those tomorrows would be met together. After awhile, they went into the house and played a trio on their instruments. They played and time crept on. For the moment, it was the only comfort available. Music not only soothes the savage beast, it calms the restless spirit. *Music is the art which is most nigh to tears and memory.* — Oscar Wilde

Music rising — music falling —
      Sweetest dream of melody!
In its soft, harmonious swelling,
      Bringing rapture unto me.

Bringing rapture, keenest rapture —
      Rapture most like agony;
Like a prophecy of evil,
      Telling of what was to be.

Telling of a time yet coming,
      When the roses should be dead;
When the music should be silent,
      And the sky be dark o'er head.

Of a time when I should wander
      Through the garden walks alone;
And the very breeze be silent,
      That in former days had blown.

Dead Dreams
Elizabeth Kantz

Echo in the Heart

* * *

Five

The mature Christmas trees had to be cut and transported to the farm's established markets. The women had to hire extra help as they could not do the physical labor the husbands used to do. Actually, it was beneficial they were involved in closely overseeing this concentrated activity and handling the accounts so that their minds could not linger too long over the fresh sad memories.

The evenings were the most difficult to endure. Daytime activities, including musical endeavors, kept the women occupied in body and mind. The early onset of darkness, when they all would at this time of the year sit by the first of many blazing fires in the massive fireplace in the den and play cards, word games, or just converse about books, the happenings of the farm, and the lives of their children, left a painful void.

They had put a bench by the graves. It was a simple structure, as the men would have liked it, just two log sections turned on end and a plank board stretched across to each. They would bundle up on chilly days and spend time sitting there in that serene setting. It was a way of staying close and keeping hold on the thoughts of those fulfilling times gone by. A foreboding quiet would surround them, and the faint echo in the heart could barely be detected.

Autumn comes early to the mountains. Leaves turn vivid colors well before those in the lowlands. The high country also has an earlier frost. The changing of the seasons, so pronounced around them, was one of the special features they all loved about their home.

One early November morning, Wendy went on her usual morning walk up the lane, the long drive from the house to the main highway. A movement in the bushes caught her eye. Cautiously, she approached the spot. To her amazement, a pair of coal black eyes peered out at her. It was a small dog, its fur badly matted and appallingly malnourished. She took off her wool-lined jacket and placed it around the shivering animal, a grateful whimper coming from the trembling body. Wrapped in the jacket, Wendy walked briskly back to the house with her discovery, thinking back on the two border collies they used to have on the farm going in and out of the house at will. The children loved the dogs and until they had to put them to sleep because of old-age ailments they had been loving members of the family.

Regina and Candy were in the kitchen sipping coffee when Wendy rushed in with the bundle. They gasped at the emaciated condition of the poor animal. People are known to abandon unwanted pets in the country, and they could only speculate that some callous person had dumped the dog at or near the entrance to their lane. If persons are cruel to animals their treatment of people is bound to be just as bad. The women never could tolerate cruelness in any manner. They shied away from folks who did unkind acts.

They took the dog to the local veterinarian they had used for the border collies. She diagnosed the dog as dehydrated and badly malnourished but otherwise of apparent good health. The age was guessed at of about a year old, and a mix of breeds, probably of a beagle and a terrier. The dog was kept overnight and put on special fluids. This gave the women a chance to stock up on dog food and to take out one of the dog beds they still had in the storeroom and set a place for the new arrival in a corner of the utility room.

They brought the dog home the following afternoon, and he already looked better and was frisky. They named him Adagio, although he was anything but slow moving now that he was substantiated. After a good bath and clipping, he looked adorable and it was mind-boggling how anyone could give him up without seeking a good home for him.

Adagio was eager to be trained, and in no time at all he had full run of the house, indicated when he needed to be taken out, and his bed was moved into the warmer and cozier kitchen. What especially endeared the pooch to the members of the house was how he lay still at their feet when they played their instruments. Could music be in the soul of a dog?

One brisk afternoon the three sauntered over to the bench, Adagio sticking close by with no need for a leash. For a few moments they sat in silence, personal thoughts leading to a highway of memories.

Candy cleared her throat. "I have been thinking of something for a couple of days. It is time I ran it by you both since it is an idea that deserves some discussion. As I look back over the years, so many ideas have been prime topics for a hashing." She grew silent as the other two women gazed in her direction. "I believe Adagio has come into our lives for a reason, to lead us to a new purpose. Since losing the currency of our lives, I believe a new venture is essential to enable us to go on. A vital purpose to fill part of the void of our existence." She grew silent again.

Regina was tempted to urge Candy to come out with it already, but she knew better than to rush the woman who had always been pensive and deliberate in describing any contemplated action. Of the three, Candy's hesitation had served them well over the years.

"While we were at the Vet's office, one of the assistants told me that the number of neglected strays has been escalating since economic times have been hard. My heart pours out to these poor victims of cruel neglect, intentional or otherwise. We have plenty of room here, and we need to fill our lives with a new purpose. I propose we create a no-kill dog shelter."

Regina and Wendy were at first speechless. Not that they would have guessed what Candy's proposal might be, but the idea was the furthest thing from their minds.

"I can tell this must have been brewing in your mind for a spell," Wendy offered. "It is not an overnight plan. It is not the kind of scheme we can start and then drop it. It is a huge commitment. These are living creatures who may need more than we may be able to give them."

"I have thought it all out. We can handle it. We need not establish a gigantic undertaking. Perhaps, just a couple dozen of the most needy dogs, ones no one apparently will ever want. To spare them from being euthanized will be its own reward. Just think of the rich feeling of making each of their remaining days as wonderful as possible. We can certainly afford to do this and where we may be lacking I am sure animal lovers will contribute to such a worthwhile cause. Remember when we insulated and heated and air-conditioned the storeroom out back so that we could keep our spare instruments there? Of course, it is chock full of other things which we can move out to the barn. It won't take much to convert it to a place to house those pitiful creatures, and with easy access from the house we can take turns caring for them. My heart goes out to them."

Regina was usually the one with the most reserve. She smiled broadly before speaking. "I should have known you would come up with a plan that encompasses so much of our time, energy, and finances. I like the idea, but let's give it some time to come up with some negatives other than the obvious ones. Do you remember our old handyman, Mike, who would always want to dwell on a project before he undertook it. He described it as letting something bake in the oven first. So, let it bake until we know it is truly for us."

Candy raised an eyebrow. "What negatives?"

"Like distracting from the business we already run here, our music, our reading, and time with our grandchild and the other grandchildren bound to come along." Regina wanted to mention the time as the present when they could leisurely sit on the bench and feel closeness to their husbands. She thought it best to concentrate on the tangibles, liking the idea but not completely sold on it. "We also need to look into what licensing, insurance, and other legal requirements may exist."

Wendy's frown was an indication of some doubt. "We have been through a good deal of emotional torment. I am not sure I can handle a situation such as with Adagio multiplied many fold. There will be dogs that cannot be saved even with what we might be able to offer. I am not sure I can bear repeated losses, especially death situations that will bring our own personal tragedies up over and over again. One thing I have learned recently. I am not emotionally strong enough to adjust to death situations."

"That's a valid point, my dear Wendy," Regina stated emphatically. "All the more reason to think this through and for us to come to terms with what this kind of undertaking entails. We have the luxury of deliberation, so let's take full advantage of it. As with so many of the other features of our lives, past, present, and future, it is no good unless we are all in agreement and approach it together."

"I did not mean that this has to be." Candy's voice had a twinge of disappointment in it. "I just know that the doing of such good will make us all feel good. If the men were here, I believe they would be in favor of such a plan."

They returned to the house and gravitated towards their instruments. So many emotions were now pulling them in seemingly different directions. Music, the savior of so many events in their lives, has the magic to soothe the disquiet of restless thoughts. They would look at Adagio lying so calmly at their feet, and he would play an instrument along with them if he could. Of this, they were certain.

Later that night, it was decided that since Thanksgiving was at hand and all of the children would be home, the idea would be brought up then for a family discussion. The input of the children would be valuable. After all, if such an idea came to fruition it would have an impact on them as well. If it became a reality, all of the farm activities other than the Christmas trees would have to be curtailed or fall by the wayside. If it was meant to be, it had to be a complete commitment. There would be no way to accept and care for rejected dogs and then abandon them again. Ideas involving living creatures take on a finality by virtue of the nature of its scope. A lifetime commitment to music emphasizes that certain endeavors are ongoing, and rightly so.

Forgetting the past — with its dreams
That faded away
Like the radiant dazzling colors of sunset
That came not to stay.

The fleecy white clouds — you fancied
Were castles most fair
With towers and turrets — with banners of sunbeams
Afloat in the air.

Forgetting the past — with its dreams
Like tales that are told,
Dream dreams brighter — fairer than ever before
In years now grown old.

New Year Fancies
Grace Hibbard

* * *

Six

Adagio was a bundle of excitement as each of the children arrived for the holiday. He thrived on attention, and Eve was particularly taken with him and carried him around as if he was a doll. A note of sadness prevailed with the feeling that the family was not whole and never could be again. Yet, the warmth of loved ones being together and sharing stories and playing music was a form of fulfillment. In a way, it was a tribute to the men and the substance of what they had left behind.

At dinner the night before Thanksgiving, the mothers raised the possibility of creating a no-kill dog shelter at the farm. It did prompt a good deal of discussion that carried on after the meal when they congregated in the den. Basically, the youngsters were all in agreement that it was a noble idea and that involvement would be beneficial for their mothers, but they were hesitant to give a full go-ahead approval. Thankful that they were consulted, they all felt that since they were no longer at the farm any final decision had to rest solely with the mothers. It was probably what they anticipated the reaction would be. Reasonable and caring children are the harvest of loving parents.

Adam, as an accountant, made the soundest suggestion. He proposed that they contact some existing shelters, even in other states, to find out what is really involved in running such a place, especially the negatives. Then, they should get some estimates in converting the storeroom to an animal housing facility. Perhaps, that cost alone might make the venture prohibitive.

The Internet was overflowing with information, some of it useless and conflicting, but there was enough insight and reports of experiences to help evaluate the proposal. A few telephone calls interviewing some shelter managers, and a personal visit by Candy to a shelter in Chattanooga, and they had a pad full of notes to wade through. The Jensen brothers, who had built the barn, priced out converting the storeroom using cages that could be ordered already assembled. The trickiest part would be to run a water supply to the room, as well as adding some windows, skylights, and a back door. The final estimate while high was not a deterrent.

All of this was put aside as they prepared for Christmas. The house had to be decorated, including using the wreaths they made. The children arrived a few days early so that the family musical ensemble might practice. They were to be part of the Christmas Eve program at the Civic Center, and they were to play some classic Christmas songs and an excerpt from the Nutcracker Suite. Eve would ring a hand bell at Helene's signal throughout the playing.

After the children arrived, they all went out into the field and let Eve choose a Christmas tree to cut and be placed in the den. In spite of the tragic events of the past year, the time was festive and all were intent on making it that way, especially for Eve. The quiet moments, however, were laden with longing and vivid memories.

On Christmas morning a light snow covered the countryside, and was a beautiful setting for a family time. A fire blazed in the large stone fireplace, and presents were opened followed by a feast of various foods that had been a combined effort of nearly all there. While the family was not complete, the magic of Christmas combined with the familiar protocol, fostered a renewed spirit. The echo in the heart while dim was still vibrant.

After New Year's Day when the women were once again alone, they sat at the picnic table in the kitchen to hash out the idea about the dog shelter. Candy shuffled through her notes. "One thing is for sure. There's more to this than I first envisioned, but I am convinced it can be done. Do we want it done? That, dear sisters of my heart, is the million-dollar question. I look at Adagio and see what we can do and that is enough persuasion for me. He has a second chance at a quality life. But, I am the impetuous one of this trio. We all need to be fully behind this. We cannot deny that the cause is worthwhile, but should it be our cause? If it is, will we feel that way after going through the effort and expense of creating the shelter, including imposing vet bills, licenses and inspections by both the State and County, insurance, and food, just to name a few considerations."

Wendy interrupted her. "There is another thing we have failed to mention before. We thrive on the quiet here both for our own peace of mind and for the playing of music. How will the howling of lonely and sick dogs infringe on an existence we are so accustomed to?"

Candy turned to her. "That's a good point. Yet, with this and some other features known and perhaps yet unknown, we will not know how we will react or adjust until they happen. Ginny, cool-headed Regina, give us your wisdom."

"If only I was wise enough to be sure of anything anymore. The only thing I am sure of is without the two of you there is no reason to tackle any demanding venture. I want for us to do it if only because the compelling need is there, and what few dogs we may be able to add a promise for a better tomorrow than their yesterdays, to alleviate the suffering, is a purpose not out of line with the design of our entire lives. I think of it in terms of a dog commune."

Cindy chuckled. "Well, that's two for the idea. Wendy, the decision rests with you."

"Thanks a lot. I detest playing the role of the spoiler, so let's do it."

They hugged and then went out to the bench to tell the men of their newly espoused cause. It was a time to reflect and to look forward to a major challenge.

By the third week of April, the JAF (John Archer Freeman) Dog Shelter had been established, and by mid-May there were seven canine occupants. The veterinarian and a flattering article in the local weekly newspaper primarily spread the word. Adagio was ensconced as the household pet, so he just appraised the operation as a distraction from his kitchen time.

The seven dogs in residence were mixed breeds of varying ages most likely difficult to pinpoint. Their health conditions ranged from poor to grave, and initial medical attention was expensive (even with a sympathetic discount) and time-consuming. Two of the dogs had already been neutered, and the others would have to be so if their conditions improved. Each of the stories was sad to hear and sadder to ponder over. One barely escaped an intentional fire; another was locked for a long time in a dark shed with little food and water; one was tortured; one was used for target practice; one was mercilessly beaten; one was badly mangled from being hit by a car; and another purposely blinded.

Day and night care prevailed, and just exercising the ones able to walk outside was a prolonged effort. None of them would admit that they might have bitten off more than they could chew as the number and needs of the dogs escalated. This plight was readily admitted when the children called to inquire on the progress.

That honest admission to the children did trigger an interesting development. Because of the ever-constricting economy and the shrinking real estate market, Felicia lost her banking broker job. Instead of looking for a new one, she decided to move back home and help with the shelter. Mandy, who never did care for the firm at which she squandered her secretarial functions, quit her job and joined her sister in the homeward bound quest. There were only two months remaining on their lease, and a rental truck was adequate to transport their sparse furniture. Open arms were awaiting them. The once distant echo in the heart grew in intensity.

Spring turned into summer, and all of the children assembled to mark the first anniversary of the deaths of their fathers. Wendy read Emily Bronte's poem "Remembrance":

> No other sun has lighted my heaven,
> No other star has ever shone for me;
> All my life's bliss from thy dear life was given,
> All my life's bliss is in the grave with thee.

Then Candy and Regina took turns reciting the poignant poem "With You a Part of Me," by George Santayana:

> With you a part of me hath passed away;
> For in the peopled forest of my mind
> A tree made leafless by this wintry wind
> Shall never don again its green array.
> Chapel and fireside, country road and bay,
> Have something of their friendliness resigned;
> Another, if I would, I could not find,
> And I am grown much older in a day.
> But yet I treasure in my memory
> Your gift of charity, and young heart's ease,
> And the dear honor of your amity;
> For these once more, my life is rich with these,
> And I scarce know which part may greater be—
> What I keep of you, or you rob from me.

A heavy silence hung over the gathering. Handholding and hugging seemed the only way to foster a transition between what had been lost and what still remained. Tears accompanied the slow walk back to the house.

The children, upon seeing the demanding undertaking of the shelter first hand where the occupants now numbered eighteen, sparked the impetus for a decision that had already been under serious consideration. Ricky and Jean wanted to move back and assist in the operation. Jean had already left her job, as she was eight months pregnant. Ricky had rationalized that his helping people as a psychoanalyst would bring the same satisfaction if he helped animals. He could always return to his chosen field at a later time.

The baby arrived a week early. The boy was named John after his grandfather, the nickname John-John popping up almost immediately as he was the second John. Having a new baby in the home was a delightful involvement for all of the members of the household.

The expectation for Adam and Helene to round out the completeness of the family in this enterprise was rising. All assured them that there were now enough hands at home to handle the venture and they should only decide what was best for them. Yet, the draw of family was too strong, and within a month they, with Eve in tow, came back to the fold. Until the Jensen brothers finished an addition to the house, things were a bit cramped, except for kitchen and den time where the rooms were big enough to accommodate all. Barking dogs, a baby crying, and scurrying activity were constant reminders there was a full house.

At one point, the decision had to be made whether cats should also be harbored at the shelter. Besides the space problem, reluctantly they concluded to limit the entry to dogs. More and more time was being consumed trying to get the ones adopted when restored to fairly good health. As mountain jargon would have it, it would only be a miracle if any of the dogs would become as lively as a Mississippi squirrel. Showing the dogs, interviews, and home visits became major actions. Hearts were gladdened with the first adoption, but even this was tinged by the sadness that most of the others might never get to that point. Giving them quiet and comfortable final days with the love of the host family surrounding them might be the best there could ever be.

Eve and John-John filled the house with the squeals of new life and fresh love. Each day brought the exhausted adults to one satisfying result. The caring and putting that caring into action are the golden strands of life.

"Why search for flowers anymore?" she said,
    Turning aside to leave the quiet wood;
Yet all undaunted her companion stood,
A shaft of sunlight falling on her head.
    "For me no flowers ever bloom!" she cried;
    "Always and ever have I looked in vain!
    Only the dull brown leaves like leaves of pain
    Drifting around my feet from every side!"
    "Nay, dear," the other answered tenderly,
    "Standing in the shadowy place;
Under the leaves some flowers there may be,
Or some shy buds that promise all things sweet."
    And kneeling, with a smile upon her face,
Uncovered blossoms at her very feet.

Under the Leaves
Jean Kate Ludlum

Seven

By the middle of the summer, there were twenty-seven dogs in the shelter. The family was reluctant to have to turn dogs away but there was just no other choice. A few were now near good condition so that adoption might be feasible, although that procedure was still slow and uncertain. The time was also drawing near for the mature Christmas trees to be cut and seedlings planted in their place.

With all of the willing resident help, Regina, Wendy, and Candy often had a chance to sit on the bench by the pond or on the porch rockers. On one tranquil night they were gently rocking in the chairs. All of the dogs had been settled in for the night, and they could barely hear the television in the den.

Candy was particularly ebullient after Helene's announcement at dinner that she and Adam were expecting another child. "I suppose I should now finally compose that Grandmother's Symphony that I have had in mind. A joyous musical treat for sure, but it will not make me feel any younger."

"Ah, we have a lot to show for our years," Wendy offered pensively.

Regina joined in, "Sounds like a pity party is forming as you think our lives are ending. We have a good deal of living yet to do, and many reasons to keep living a vibrant existence."

"I did not mean to sound fatalistic," Candy spoke slowly. "The reasons do keep increasing for us to be around. I suppose I just dread the time which may come sooner than we may expect and want, when ill health or death shall separate us."

Regina snapped back, "Yes, we can and should recognize the fragility of life and have experienced that already first hand. Yet, we cannot live our days worrying about whether or not there will be a tomorrow. Our coffers are filled to the brim with the riches that multiple lifetimes can supply. Our friendship, our family, and our music are all edifices of magnificence and strength. They are castles in the sky. They are palaces for others to gawk at."

Wendy went to the den, retrieved a book and read aloud what she thought most appropriate, a thought by Epicurus: We must meditate on the things that make us happy. *When one grows old, one may be young in blessings through the recollection of what has been. In youth, one may be old as well since one will know no fear of what is to come.*

"O.K.," Candy conceded. "I get the point. Let's just hold hands as we used to around the campfire. That will warm my soul and nourish my will."

They held hands, gently rocking as minutes turned into an hour. Fatigue could not obscure the significance of a friendship that was unshakeable. That alone is a lifetime.

Arrangements had been finalized for the family musical ensemble to give a concert at the Civic Center to raise money for the shelter. Since the family played together nearly every day no extended rehearsals would be necessary. Little did Regina know when she went to town to pick up the concert posters at the printer that a new adventure awaited them.

She went around town asking shopkeepers to put a poster in their storefront windows. One stop was at the Senior Citizen's Center, and they put a poster prominently on the bulletin board in the lobby. While there, a local author, Daniel Hill Zafren, was holding a book signing for his seventh novel that had been recently published. The signing was held there since that book was a touching story about some elderly folks. She chatted with him for about half an hour, and after Regina recited how much each member of the family loved to read, Dan suggested that they form a family book club. As a start, he proposed to sell them each at discount a copy of his first book, *In a World We Never Made.* After they all had read it, marked it up as they saw fit and discussed it among themselves, since he did not live too far away he offered to come over and answer questions about the book and give them an author's insight into the writing.

Regina thought this to be a wonderful idea. It would be an engrossing family involvement and a distraction from the work of the shelter and farm. An added benefit arose when Dan noted that his wife, Valarie, had volunteered extensively at a no-kill shelter in West Virginia when they lived there and would probably love to spend some quality time with the dogs. Regina insisted Dan and Valarie come for dinner the following evening. Dan could bring the books and one of the family would show them the animal shelter operation.

Each member thought the book club was a splendid idea, and that it would be an interesting and unusual form of intellectual entertainment. At their request, Regina telephoned Dan to make sure he signed a copy of the book for each reader.

After arriving for the dinner, Adam first showed Dan and Valarie the shelter, many of the dogs coming to the front of their cages to smell her hand. Valarie offered to come over for a few hours a couple of days a week to help out. Adam told her that walking the dogs able to be exercised would be a tremendous help. The dogs loved to be walked through the acres of Christmas trees. Assistance with the adoption process would also be wonderful.

As they sat around in the den after dinner, Eve and John-John tucked in for the night, Dan distributed copies of his first novel, *In a World We Never Made*. "I hope you will find the book absorbing, although it is not an easy book to read. My later books are easier, I promise. Trudge through the first two chapters. What you may find particularly intriguing if you keep on reading my books is to see how I develop as a writer and how the books evolve. When I wrote this first one, I had no intention of their being any later books. You be the judge. Maybe I tried to put too much into it. One of my books is a murder mystery, and that falls in a class of its own. This one is primarily a book about ideas, and that is why it is described as a scholarly novel. The story and characters are used to bring forth the ideas and expound on them. The later books still deal with ideas either in the abstract or as moral lessons of life, but the story and characters are more pronounced. Whenever you are ready and feel comfortable that a discussion with the author will clarify aspects of the book, I will be delighted to meet with you. There is nothing an author likes better than to talk about his writings. One caveat, do not hold back any punches. I don't expect everyone to love my books, and weaknesses and faults enable me to become a better writer. A thoughtful reader can easily have comments and questions. A line by Bacon is fitting: *Some books are to be tasted, others to be swallowed, and some few to be chewed and digested.* Since you have your own copies, mark them up as you see fit, even if it is just to read aloud a passage that you may have found especially appealing or disturbing. The main thing is that this should be an enjoyable undertaking. Don't look on it as a chore. Have fun, and we'll share in the good times."

While the fog o'er hangs the ocean,
    Ships bewildered ride the foam,
When it lifts they find their bearings
    And the breezes speed them home;
So from mists of doubtful seeming
    Mind will languish to be free,
Only as its insight clears up
    Can its outlook cross the sea
Fill the soul with inspiration
    To attain its destiny.

Looking Outward
T. Park Bucher

Eight

The concert was sold out. Dan and Valarie babysat for Eve and John-John and kept an eye on the dogs while the concert was being held. When the family returned, they were extremely satisfied with the performance and the amount of money raised. Some discussion ensued about expanding the size of the shelter, although too many reasons surfaced against such an action. Mainly, they thought they would not be able to devote enough attention to each animal if the number increased. The future was also uncertain.

One cool late summer morning, the women walked without speaking down the lane with Adagio sprinting along and sniffing every vegetation. On the way back they sat on the bench overlooking the graves, the pond and the beginning expanse of the Christmas trees. Regina was the first one to utter what was on all of their minds. "I feel badly about not helping as many dogs as we can. Yet, we are not getting any younger and it is very demanding work. I know we would find it to be a hardship to take on additional responsibilities."

"Our plate is already overflowing," Wendy offered.

"I know this sounds cruel," Candy interjected, "But we know it is difficult even now to give full personal attention to each dog we have. To have more and they'll just become a mass, a blur before our eyes. And, when would it end? So many dogs need help. There is so much suffering because of bad people and bad times. If we were to take on more, it would not end there. We might not be able to control it."

"Well put," Regina commented. "Plus, there would be the added pressure on the children to stay. We owe it to them to encourage them to find their own way, their own lives. Maybe encourage is too strong a word. We just need to make sure they are not irrevocably bound to this place because of what we do."

"Right," Candy continued, "We made that kind of freedom for ourselves and they deserve no less. On a more selfish note, what about us? Our deserving days are not over, not by a long shot. I am about halfway through with Dan's book, and I think it is opening up my eyes that we need more out of life than we have for our personal well being. It is not a detraction from our husbands, but before life completely passes us by I think we need some romance. I miss being held in bed at night, and I miss a man's special attention." Her voice trailed off, almost as if she had already said too much.

They were quiet for a few minutes. Wendy blurted out, "What man would be interested in a woman our age, immersed in farm labor and animal salvation?"

Candy smiled sheepishly. "We won't know unless we try."

"You were the man-seeker in our young days," Wendy grinned. "Do you think you can do it again?"

"Why not? Anything and everything is possible, I say. What do you say, Ginny?"

"I think you should leave me out of this. Frankly, romance is the furthest thing from my mind. I have had a life with a loving husband, cruelly cut short, but it along with our friendship has me fulfilled. By all means, follow your hearts. I do not want to influence you. Just promise me that you will stay close by. I am not sure I could tolerate even one of you moving away."

"That's not an option," Wendy said sternly. "It's a tall order, but a man would have to be kind, gentle, a non-smoker, love dogs and music, not be afraid of hard work, and would be willing to live here with all of the sisters of the heart. We have been together too long to be separated now. Besides, I do not want to ever be apart from you two. We are emotional Siamese triplets."

Candy nodded in frantic agreement. "That goes for me double. We discovered long ago that we are weak apart and invincible together. Who in their right mind would want to change that?"

Regina smiled cunningly. "This sure will prove to be interesting. I can't wait to see what comes crawling out when you beat the woodwork."

"I am not sure we should mention this to the children." Wendy grew silent for a moment. "They would probably be alright with it, but it could be seen as disloyalty to their fathers. Anyway, it may never come to pass, and one of the things we have learned over the course of our lives is not to raise red flags unnecessarily."

"Precisely," Candy pronounced with a tone of authority.

Regina grinned. "I'm going to have a good time being a casual observer to this circus. Tell the men to take a number so they can wait their turn. We can feed the rejects to the dogs."

"Very funny," Candy responded. "We have taken many risks in our lives, the latest being the dog shelter. This is just one more risk. One thing is clear. If we are not open to new ideas and not receptive to change, opportunities slip by unnoticed."

Regina stood, shaking out the stiffness in her body that she felt more these days. "That's a good line. I think you should share it with Dan so he can put it in one of his books."

"Maybe, he already has."

They headed back to the house and a cup of fresh coffee in the kitchen. Some play time with Eve, tending to the dogs, and it would be lunchtime with family togetherness. Knowing glances brought extra smiles.

Unloved, and loving no one, human life
Is narrowed to the petty sphere of self;
Like archer's arrow, featherless, it may
Make upward flight, but cannot pierce the cross,
And win the golden prize of happiness.
True life begins when love has warmed the heart —
A two-fold life, a mystic twain in one,
Wherein we cannot tell which one is self —
A life in which the me is lost in thee,
And where the rule by which we judge each word
And deed reads, "I am not my own but thine" —

Love Light
Wingard

Echo in the Heart

* * *

Nine

They all finished reading Dan's first book, *In a World We Never Made*, and decided to save any discussion on it until Dan was present. The interesting feature of having the author around was worth waiting for.

With all assembled in the den one Friday evening, Dan was the first to speak. "In hopeful anticipation, I have copies of my second book in the car. *A Door Never Opened* is a stand-alone sequel to the one you have just read. Stand-alone means you can read it without ever having read the first one, but it has greater meaning if the first one has been read. *In a World We Never Made*, as you know, took place in 1974. In the sequel some of the same main characters are found in a present day setting. I also devised a way of working in some poems my father had written to my mother, and I was able to employ the device of a book within a book."

Jean nervously interrupted him. "I hope there are proverbs in it. I just love proverbs, and I read and reread the ones here just to savor how deep meanings can be captured in so few words."

"There are, so you have an additional element to look forward to."

"Good. And, as long as I have in a way opened the discussion, you were right about the beginning of the book being not easy to read. Yet, I think it amply set the stage for what follows."

"I actually broke a cardinal rule of writing fiction. A writer is supposed to make the beginning easy to read and tempting in design so that the reader will want to read on. Writing fiction is very different from writing in the business world. There, sentences need to be short and to the point. They say if you have to read a sentence twice it is no good. A writer of fiction has the luxury to develop a style that very well may include sentences that lead the reader to read them twice to gather in all of the wisdom and nuances. I hope there were parts in this book that made you have to do that."

"Not just sentences," Ricky interjected, "Entire paragraphs."

"I had to read a couple of chapters twice," Wendy offered. "I love the way you write, and I thought the book was wonderful. It certainly held my attention. I kept thinking of Virginia Woolf's observation that a great novel creates the world anew for a good reader."

"I thought you captured the essence of those times well," Candy spoke slowly. "Wendy, Ginny, and I were in high school through most of the antiwar sentiment, and it reached into the beginning of our college years. In fact, when I met my husband, Archer, he was the President of the Students for Democratic Action. My young radical leader had so much fire. He was ready to set the world ablaze for change. He mellowed over the years, but he was always super critical of any strict dictates of society that coerced people to be other than what they wanted to be. It was even the impetus for our starting the communal living here, resulting in the closeness of our burgeoning family. If Archer were here, there would be so much in your book that he could identify with. It would have brought back memories of a time, just as in the book with Ted Amherst, when society was an enemy. Of course, Ted did have a revelation of sorts but was already trapped in a role he apparently had to play out. I thought that whole scenario accentuated the theme of your book."

"Which is?"

"Pretty obvious as it emerges more than once. Trying to belong to the youth movement just to fit in is no different than conforming to the expectations of the rest of society. One can belong to both, but the person can and should not lose the individual wants and needs. In the midst of all of the currents pulling him in various directions, a person can make a niche to satisfy that individuality and be truly his own person."

"Well put, Candy. It is so gratifying to hear your summary."

"It's easy," Regina broke in. "Since we have done just that in our communal type of living. Being involved with music is also an avenue of self-expression. Playing music is one thing, feeling it is another world."

Dan could not help the smile that came to his lips. Having readers relate his philosophy to their own lives is most gratifying. "Any comments on the characters?"

Helene cleared her throat. "I think the character you developed the best was Dr. Mington. He was not a likeable person, but you succeeded in making his torment so real. I imagine many people have dark places that intrude on their contentment. It is just, I hope, that most do not let it rule their conduct."

Wendy spoke up. "I liked Kate. I was hoping that Justin would have wound up with her. They had so much in common. I am not sure I fully grasped why he chose Estelle."

"It is obvious if you think of it with his mind. So much of Estelle represented similarities with his early love that he could not deny her strong love for him. He had done that once and had paid a heavy price ever since. If you will recall, besides writing his new book, the reason Justin was at the university was to find a love like he had or at least to come to an understanding why he had lost it."

"The person I felt most sorry for," Jean began, "Was Rita. She had to bear so much pain for a youngster, more pain than anyone at any age should have to live with. I could well relate to why she latched on to Justin as a savior. I would like for you to have spent more time with her thoughts and turmoil, although I realize you can do just so much in a book. I hope she is in the sequel."

"You'll see. It's a tough choice for an author when multiple characters are involved in a story. If you go too much on a tangent with one that might easily be a book in itself. Too little might be confusing or leave a reader, such as yourself, wanting more. It comes down to a choice that has to be made pretty much on the spot, and only later thinking and reader reaction can provide a resolution as to whether a right choice was made. It just seems that during the writing I had to proceed with what appeared best for the total plot and design of the book."

"I especially liked the last paragraph," Mandy commented. "I thought it was right to the point and, of course, since our home is extra special we actually have a place where our individuality has always blossomed. The family unit is unique in this disjointed world and shines bright."

"Sometimes I think my sister and I are twins since our reactions are often alike." Felicia flashed a broad smile at Mandy.

"Well," Dan began, "That is also my favorite paragraph. And, since I feel it conveys so much I actually repeat it in the sequel which, if you decide to proceed with, you will discover how I managed to do that."

"By all means," Regina and Wendy said nearly in unison.

"The first paragraph is also a favorite of mine. Writers find it particularly challenging to come up with a captivating opening. You might look out for that in all of the later books. In fact, there are national contests for opening lines. Let me go to the car and get copies of *A Door Never Opened* and I'll sign them for each of you."

After Dan left, all agreed it was a unique experience having the author present to field questions and receive comments. How often do we read a book and ask ourselves *What did the author really mean by that? Why did the author go one way when I expected it to go another?* It is also an eye-opening experience for an author to discover that a reader may have seen something quite apart in a portion of the book than what was intended. A win-win situation.

Alone! Ah, yes, alone, too soon she found
Herself far out, above, beyond the bound
Where the prudent venture in their timid quest;
She walked alone — had distanced all the rest.

Behold, her fate! Her grim reward was this:
To journey, lone, and friendly comrades miss.
O solitude! The deepest, darkest known,
Those thinkers find who strike out far alone.

Alone
Lydia Platt Richards

Ten

It was some five weeks later when they had finished reading *A Door Never Opened* and were able to meet with Dan. Ricky and Adam were involved with tending to the dogs, and as they waited for them, at Dan's prompting, the mothers related more details of their friendship as well as many of the incidences in the past. As they related such happenings, they fully realized that there was much to tell because the story was multidimensional and touching. Telling it was close to reliving it, and tears and laughter came easily. There were the times of substance and surprise, moments of accomplishments, and touches of tragedy. Although they had heard it before and had been a part of it themselves, the children listened engrossed by the underlying structure of their being.

When all were present the discussion began on *A Door Never Opened*. "Well, folks, did the sequel do its job?"

Jean grabbed the bait. "I thought it was both sad and uplifting, a good job indeed. I like how you brought the characters current, especially with the use of the dedication plaque on Henderson Hall for Kate. The saying it without really saying it."

Mandy spoke up. "I particularly liked when Ted visited Lucy. I thought you captured the mood by exploring each one's thoughts and feelings."

"I was disappointed," Helene began, "That there was nothing about Dr. Mington. I would have liked to know whether or not he was able to regain a semblance of a life."

Dan offered an explanation. "I debated about covering him in some way. Then, I thought that it might be good that not everything is laid out for the reader. Why not let the reader speculate about him?"

Helene continued, "So, what did happen to him?"

"What would you think?"

"I would suspect he eventually took his own life. After all, he was half dead already."

Wendy spoke up. "I like to think he found some purpose to sustain him in what had to be a very simple existence."

Dan raised an eyebrow. "Proves my point. It sure is interesting for an author to realize that at times what he has not put in the book can be as thought provoking as what is in it."

"Oh," Regina bellowed, "We are just getting started, writer man. I understand why you put the book within the book. It was a vehicle for airing Justin's torment and how he resolved it without needing or wanting to finish writing it. It was also very clever to have Brandon discover the unfinished book. There was no way he could know that Justin was not going to finish it. As a tribute to him, Brandon devised what he thought was a suitable ending. Yet, it was a bit hard to follow, and in a way it encroached on the message of the rest of the book."

"I don't agree with that," Candy urged. "I found it extremely fascinating as a romantic story. We must remember that it is just a story."

"Which brings to the forefront the important and perhaps most personal question, dear author." Helene crossed her arms over the swollen belly seething with new life. "Was Justin's early love your early love? Did such a person and relationship actually exist or is it all just the figment of an overactive romantic imagination?"

"Ah," Dan began, "I was half expecting that sort of question when we talked about book number one. Let me put it to rest by confessing that it is a combination of the two. It is based on fact and embellished on by distant exaggerated memories intermingled with a mind traveling on cross currents where course and destination are unclear."

"Boy, you talked your way out of that," Adam exclaimed. "And, I am not sure if you answered it at all."

"An occupational asset and necessity."

Jean picked up on the thread. "Speaking of necessity, was it really necessary for the parents to die?"

Wendy answered for Dan. "The rest of the story would not have fallen into place so logically after that. We know better than most how sudden deaths can be traumatic. Yet, I thought it was a clear bridge between the first half of the story and the second half."

"Thank you, counselor," Dan smiled.

"You are welcome."

Jean spoke again. "Once more I enjoyed the proverbs and the sayings.

More to come, I hope."

"Now and again, but certainly not as many. You can look forward to sayings and poems at random times."

"Speaking of poems," Regina chimed in, "Your father's poems are wonderful. I can see where you derive your romantic inclination."

"I am sorry he was not alive to see this particular book or, as a matter of fact, any of my books. Does anybody have a special portion of the book that you would like to read aloud?"

Mandy opened her copy of the book. "What struck home for me was in Justin's projection of some of the things he would have said if the seminar had continued.

> *The human potential — infinite and indefatigable.*
> *As one satisfies hunger with food, the inner need*
> *for reaching as far as possible in the spectrum of*
> *the soul to experience the contentment and pride*
> *of doing the best one can. To reach the outer*
> *limits of one's capabilities. To satisfy the civilized*
> *beliefs of accomplishing deeds to better the world*
> *around us. To read and act out the story within*
> *ourselves."*

Ricky opened his copy of the book to a marked page. "I was entranced by Brandon's thoughts about young people and their growing dilemma.

> *The trip to maturity need not be a continuing*
> *struggle. It need not be rushed. There may be*
> *only one distant destination, which may not*
> *be as important as the series of steps one*
> *reaches along the way. Some of these points*
> *can be planned; many merely are the products*
> *of the journey. The most important aspect is*
> *to recognize the junctures and to consider them*

pondering points. Places to rest, to regroup,
and to dwell upon the fruits of the mental labor
exerted to reach that resting place or crossroad.
What does it mean for the moment? How can it
best be employed to build on past pondering
points? How can it ease and direct the steps to
follow? A most important lesson to learn is that
there is nothing shameful, or necessarily a sign
of weakness or failure, in taking a step backwards.
At times, that might be the best vantage point to
see the future course of action in a clearer and
more meaningful manner. Equally important,
the reality that the long term goal may truly never
be reached or even that it is not actually necessary
to be attained. A particular pondering point may
turn out to be the most satisfying, the most
fulfilling."

"Thank you, Ricky. I was at an author's workshop recently, and the authors were asked to read a brief portion of their writings they found most satisfying. That was just the excerpt I chose to read."

The discussion wound down, and Dan signed the copies of his third book *Shadow Selves*. As he left, he enjoyed the warm feeling the family had generated about his book. He liked to think he had become an honorary member of a very special family. Maybe their tantalizing story would be a future book.

No sooner doth one song depart,
In fancy's realm to soar,
Another stands outside my heart,
And taps upon the door.

The Muse
Robert Loveman

Eleven

It was a somber moment marking the second anniversary of the death of the men. The family gathered by the graves holding hands. There was a strong inclination to say some special words to acknowledge the sad memory, but it just seemed most appropriate to let the silence of the day reflect the mood and the memorial. A lone songbird warbled amidst the branches of the weeping willow tree, the tree crying in its own way. The bird's melody was in the nature of remorse and reflection. The symbol reverberated in the heart and added a firmer resonance to the echo. Warm hugs amidst tears absorbed the spirit of the ones lost and provided an impetus for those remaining to carry on with the deeds and principles to add meaning to their lives.

Helene gave birth to a boy, Gordon Archer Menton. Gordon was her father's name. He had died when she was a teenager. The house was filled again with the accustomed sounds of a new baby. This was another diversion away from a romantic quest. New grandma Candy sighed, "What will be will be." Extended grandma Wendy sighed, "What is is." Extended grandma Regina sighed, "I could say I told you so but I won't since I had no idea it would be so."

Candy combed the bushes and even beat the woodwork as Regina had phrased it, and still no male prospects. She even tried the Appalachian State alumni office and contacted all of the orchestras in North Carolina with discreet inquiries. There was a reluctance to use a computer dating service because of all of the inherent unknowns as well as the time and effort required. She even enlisted the assistance of Pastor Tom, the Jensen Brothers, and a host of other acquaintances to keep their eyes and ears open for any eligible men who might want to join a book club, any willing to participate in aiding abused dogs, any that might have an inkling for music appreciation, or any just willing to chat with a bunch of old broads. So far, no luck. It really did not bother her as much as she thought it might at first, and Wendy was not pressing the issue either. Perhaps, Regina had the right idea all along. Even if more is possible, being content with a relatively full life carries a strong moral message.

Now that the Christmas tree activity was over for this year, they concentrated their energies on the dogs. Eve and Adagio had become inseparable, and he even slept at the foot of her bed. Some of the other dogs which probably would never be adopted became favorites of the family members. The most touching relationship was Mandy with Dramby, short for Drambuie, an old female mixed breed that was blind and missing a leg. Dramby would pick up Mandy's scent before the fortifying sound of her voice and the scratching behind her ears began. The aged tail would wag at a frantic pace. Mandy would take her for short walks with Dramby valiantly hobbling on three legs. Dramby loved the pungent smell of the Christmas trees, and Mandy would sit with her on the bench at the end of the walk and the two would spend a peaceful time together. For an old dog this was her moment in the sun. A woman and her dog. Do you believe in magic? Mandy knew that if the time ever came for her to leave the farm and Dramby was still alive, she would take the endearing canine with her.

Whenever they played music, either as a group or individually, the door to the shelter would be left open. The pastoral sounds had a major calming result on the dogs. *Moon Music Farm* was a perpetually busy place, and everyone had a part to adapt to and a role to play. Cooperation was a paramount theme, and duplicative efforts were not wasted time or energy but rather an added benefit for the dogs and a reinforcing drive for the family. Those who love living creatures are constantly rewarded with monumental satisfaction when that love can be vented.

Because the result was so positive about the family musical ensemble at the benefit concert, the word spread throughout the region about the delightful sounds produced. Several of the posh resorts in the region started booking the family to play at weddings and other major celebrations.

It was at one of these functions that Felicia met Greg Brachton, an artist who had his own gallery in Boone. Greg was nearly twice Felicia's age, although the mutual attraction was strong from the beginning and they started to date. Greg was divorced and lived on a small farm with a studio in Banner Elk. Within seven weeks, Greg asked Felicia to move in with him, and she readily agreed. This prompted extensive family discussions on the age difference as well as the family unit once again entering an outside breakaway mode. Candy was the first to point out secretly that Greg would have been a more likely match for Wendy or herself, but the extremely liberal outlook of the family soon accepted the arrangement, especially with Felicia's assurance that she and Greg would visit the farm frequently. The more they saw and talked to Greg, the more they grew to like his demeanor and attentiveness to Felicia. What was the crowning touch was seeing Felicia happy.

One late afternoon the ladies sat on the bench bundled up against the impending autumn chill. Regina broke the pensive silence. "Dan will be here next week for the next book discussion. As events seem to be moving quickly and often beyond our control, I think we should encourage the idea that he write a book about us. It will be a lasting memory for our children and grandchildren."

Wendy grimaced. "I wonder how he will handle writing about Felicia, my daughter........I mean our daughter, living with a man and not being married to him, in sin if you will."

"You don't mean to be that judgmental I am sure," Candy urged. "Especially in light of our liberal and flexible philosophy."

"No, it is just a term of convenience."

"At some point they probably will get married if their togetherness proves beneficial," Regina added. "I don't think the age difference is relevant for what they feel. It is just I hate to think that she may spend old age alone as we are doing."

"She'll never be actually alone." Candy's voice was firm and resonant. "Just as we are not alone because we have each other, she has a close and loving family of siblings and spouses of siblings, and nephews and nieces. That is a built-in support structure. She also has us for as long as we are alive."

"I would like to see how Dan will capture that kind of essence in words," Wendy commented.

"Just as I described it, I betchya."

"No," Regina frowned, "He will embellish it with feelings, thoughts and deeds. All of that will be necessary to describe our friendship. Its significance lies deep beneath the surface. Our oath was just words. We lived it, and that is quite a different matter."

Wendy and Candy nodded in agreement. In silence they huddled together as a bracing wind kicked up. Silently, they rose to return to the house knowing that the children would have a bountiful dinner prepared. Even if no actual fire blazed in the hearth, a perpetual warm glow is there for their spirits. That too spoke volumes.

Between the pink leaves of the poet
  We thumbed for the sober and gay,
Turned under a picture — none know it —
  The roses are treasured away;
  And often when twilight is gray,
The pages are turned and I dote
  And ponder above the bouquet
Of roses you pinned on my coat.

The moths and the mildew will prey,
  And shrivel all treasures; from mote,
Minutest, I hide the bouquet
  Of roses you pinned on my coat.

Ballad to a Bouquet
Alonzo Leora Rice

Twelve

"I thought my beguiling personality was waning," Dan spoke upon seeing that Felicia was not present in the book discussion group. "Abandonment for a higher purpose is, however, pardonable."

"We'll fill her in on it all later," Adam spoke up. "She did read it, I know, and she mentioned she enjoyed it. Her aside comment on *Shadow Selves* was that she especially liked how you worked the short stories into the book."

"Speaking of the stories," Helene interposed, "I thought they were good just as the book as a whole was good. The stories are powerful lessons for life. My favorite one is *Time as Thief*."

"My favorite," Wendy picked up on the thread, "Was *Free Float*. It sort of reminded me of us at an earlier stage of our lives when a commune represented a reasonable and viable option for our future."

"Except, my dear sister of the heart," Regina butted in, "We are all still floating. It makes me think we may never stop floating. Perhaps, when the waters are truly calm we seem not to float, but the least little shock wave can set us off in any and all directions with an inability to steer. Dan, I enjoyed the book immensely. As you told us initially, the later books do reach a balance between ideas, characters, and plot. This one affected me that way. I was touched by how each character developed a sense of hope in themselves and their future, and then how each influenced the others."

Jean picked up on this thread. "I thought you did a masterful job with the two mothers. They came across as very real people. How many folks escape into their imagination? Some, as Rika's mother, finally discover that the reality of what they needed and wanted is what they had all along. Others, as with Bryant's mother, know that only through their imagination can they endure the reality they have. This comes across vividly in the book. Mr. Author, a job well done!"

"Whew, Jean, I am absolutely delighted with your observations. An author can know what is behind his writings, but when a reader hones in on it and can portray the essence, such is extremely gratifying. Thank you so much."

"The character I felt the most for was Rika's father." Ricky coughed before continuing. "He is a typical unsung hero, giving his all without any expectations or demands. I particularly liked the dialogue early in the book when he picked

Rika up at the college and she told him about Bryant."

Mandy joined in. "I thought the relationship between Bryant and Rika was vital to the book and for all of the lives they touched. I thought it was a real good read, author man! By the way, not to get too personal but do you have any nicknames?"

"That is not personal, and you are all welcome to ask me whatever you feel will elucidate my writings and me as a person. I have already probed deeply into many traits of your family members, so it is fitting and proper. Actually, I have had two nicknames during my lifetime. The first when I was a boy growing up in Brooklyn I was part of a gang. It was not a violent gang as we currently envision the term. It was more akin to a social club, although some activities and actions upon reflection and in hindsight were probably uncalled for. My gang name was Zappo. Later on, because I was identified so often as Dan Z, it gradually became Danzy. Of course, I shudder to think of the names people may have called me behind my back."

The group laughed. Candy then spoke up energetically. "And I was very taken with the gentle way you handled the love scenes. They are tastefully done and beautifully described. None of your books have contained any gratuitous sex, and I believe that is to your credit. Too many books push sex just for sex purposes."

"Another robust thank you is in order. A compliment is easy to hear and digest."

Adam started to speak slowly. "I also liked it as an historical piece not only for the movement against the Vietnam War but also advocating the rights for the disabled before major legislation was enacted to afford them those rights. After I read Rika's article espousing rights for the handicapped, I recalled a short and powerful poem I had read in high school. I wish I had kept a copy. It concerned a young girl on a bus who saw another young girl on the bus who she thought was extremely beautiful. She wished she were that girl until she got up from her seat and it was obvious that she had no legs. The girl realized that even if she was not as pretty she was blessed to have legs. I assume you had to do some research for that aspect of the book."

"Yes, I did. Unless and until one gets involved with reading about disadvantaged people it is edifying to find some wonderful and powerful writings explaining aspects that one might not otherwise think about.   There is an analogy to paintings. I have seen paintings that are enthralling by unlisted or unrecognized artists, some not even signed or with a signature that cannot be deciphered. Some of the renowned paintings are not as eye-catching to my untrained but appreciative eye and do not captivate me as well. I suppose it is similar to my books. Not everyone slobbers over them and I suspect I will always remain undiscovered. If I ever am a literary sensation, the signed books of mine that you have should bring you a tidy sum, especially after I have died."

Mandy balked, "You can't die! That would be the end of your writings. The world may not know you, but this clan contains steadfast fans. We hunger for more. What is the next book?"

"Ah, the next one is certainly a change of pace. It is a murder mystery, *Network of Death*. I think you will find it fast-moving and intriguing. No doubt it will usher in a different kind of discussion among the clan. It has been my most popular book. Many readers like a murder mystery, and this one is absorbing, even if I have to say that myself."

Candy offered one more comment. "I liked what you just said about paintings. I have made a similar observation with poetry. There is no denying the beauty and majesty of the poems by the great poets. Yet, I have discovered meaningful and lovely poetry by unknown poets."

After Dan left, Wendy turned to Candy and Regina. "It really is too bad more people have not had the involvement with Dan's books. I know I think about them long after reading them. I wish I could write like that, especially love stories."

"Yes, that is certainly true," Regina responded. "I suppose it is proof positive of the concept that you do not know what you are missing if you do not have it. And, I am sure Dan wishes he could produce the music we play and that comes so easily to us. For you in particular, Wendy, music is the voice of love."

For music's soul on aerial wings
   Hath upward soared,
Vibrating subtle welcomings
   From chord to chord,
And time with sweet suspicions rings
Of all the joys dear summer brings,
Rich prophecies of harvestings
   In blossoms stored.

The Overture
Charles H. A. Esling

Thirteen

It was two weeks before Christmas when they could all gather to converse about *Network of Death*. Even Felicia and Greg joined the group. Greg was anxious to have a say since he read all of Felicia's copies of Dan's books so far and was hooked on them.

Dan did not have to elicit an opening statement. Regina shouted right out, "We loved the book but hated the ending!"

"The end was a real shocker," Ricky interjected. "It was a masterful touch, I will give you that. The reader is lulled into an expected ending and is jolted right out of his seat."

Dan smiled. "A writer's prerogative, I say in my defense. I have yet to come across anyone who has guessed the ending. In fact, I have a real funny story about it. A friend of ours, Jane, took the book with her on a flight to Central America with her husband, Max, to visit their daughter and her family who are missionaries there. She was just finishing the book while waiting in the airport for the return flight. Upon finishing the last chapter, she yelled out *I'm going to kill him!* All heads turned in her direction. She was lucky not to have been detained by the airport security folks there."

Helene displayed a puzzled look. "Is the ending an invitation to a sequel?"

"A frequent question tossed out at me. The answer is a mystery of its own — yes and no. It could be, but if you think about it the clues are there for a resolution of the story. You can ascertain who did it and speculate why."

"The clues are what?" Mandy raised an eyebrow. "I must have missed that."

"The absence of torture and the smashed turtles."

"Oh, now I get it. Sure is obvious if someone points it out."

"Well," Adam commented, "I thought the book had everything comprising a thriller. It would make a fantastic movie. Hollywood here you go!"

"Even though the story is riveting," Helene spoke up, "I liked how you developed the characters. Besides the main folks, even in cryptic fashion I had a real feeling for each of the network women. One could empathize with Brenda.

I also thought that Howard was a well-defined character, and I thought his aside comments were a nice touch. I had to chuckle each time he saw a painting with a light illuminating it and he concluded because of that the painting must be valuable. I had a friend who had inexpensive art on her walls and she had a spotlight on each one only because she had poor eyesight. I also got a kick out of the bit about the story on a cup."

"I'm the newcomer here," Greg entered the discussion while firmly holding Felicia's hand. "I found this an exciting book, and I put my painting on hold which I rarely do while I read the others I had missed. It was certainly different as, actually, amazingly all of them are. I hope I can capture that kind of freshness in each of my paintings."

"It is distinctive but not so different," Regina offered opening up her book. "Not just a matter of semantics. While there are not as many direct ideas, they are there. One of the obvious ones is my favorite part of the book.

> A premonition is a sad song carried in the wind.
> Its melody is unrecognizable and its words
> blurred by the ghastly sounds ushering it along.
> One of those gasps in the void of time passing,
> with no beginning and no end. It is strange and
> familiar at the same moment. It carries the
> unwilling recipient to places both grand and
> puny. A scar on the heart and the mind is all
> that is left.

The scar on the heart image is personally forceful for me. My sisters of the heart know that I have equated for all of our lives that happiness and sadness are registered as an echo in the heart. I get to wondering what effect a scar on the heart would have on the echo. I can only judge from my perspective but it must be very meaningful when a reader transposes an author's description and thought to relate to a personal experience and belief."

"Right on the button, dear lady!"

"I liked the part," Wendy offered as she pulled out her copy of the book and turned to the page with a bookmark in it.

*There was plenty of time to think about his life
as he drove. He had avoided a detailed introspection,
fearful of what he would be forced to admit to himself.
Yet, such a self-analysis was long overdue. It is
probably beneficial for all people to engage in an
inward look at various stages of their lives. That
way they can place a marker on the trail they are
following. Such a marker can ease a retreat or even
accentuate the idea to take a risk or different turn when
and if the need or opportunity arises. Probably the
most crucial element is to keep the mind in motion
until enlightening discovery when a place of
contentment is arrived at. Then, the secret is not
to look back."*

Candy's comment was next. "It is obvious you did research for this as I assume what you wrote about industrial espionage is all fact."

"Yes, it is. Actually, it is a fascinating subject and I was tempted to go into even more detail but I did not want to bog the story down too much. There is no shortage of information and opinion, and it is indeed a worldwide issue. It is the subject that sparked the book. I thought sexespionage would be the area to delve into. There was also research on hate groups, another fascinating area. It is amazing to discover the range of deviant human activity. I did not want to glamorize it in any way. I think the more focus on extreme behavior the better as it can raise awareness and caution."

"Quite scary, I would say." Candy shuddered slightly. "We are accustomed here to the helpful and considerate mountain folk. High crime and sordid actions are the exception and not the general rule. I imagine there are crazies everywhere. It is just I don't want to think about it."

"That's true, unfortunately," Dan replied. "The results of a free society are not always wholesome or peaceful. One aspect that I tried to convey is that much of it is hidden by the nature of the secretiveness of such groups. It is only when they break laws is attention drawn to them. Those that are seething in the background are potentially the most dangerous."

"Not a light note with Christmas so close," Helene concluded. "Tell us about the next book. I am not sure what I will do when we run out of your books, Danzy. I am sure I will suffer intellectual withdrawal symptoms."

"I'll just have to write more books faster to keep up with you. The next one is *Not Lost — Just Not Found*. While back in a college setting, it as you may guess another different kind of story. I hope it is not a letdown from the fast-paced murder mystery which is designed to keep you guessing."

As Dan signed the next book for the family, he felt very close to them. He was thinking of them as an extended family of his own. He admired their causes, how they interacted with loving and caring, and how they persevered under trying moments. As much as he considered himself a good person, he wondered if he would still be a better one if he had been raised in a communal-type setting. Certainly, he would be a better writer.

Rain, rain, rain! How many complain,
Because of the beautiful rain;
But the grass is green, the wood path clean,
And the water shines with a silver sheen,
As on it falls the rain.

The Grateful Rain
S. M. Watson

Fourteen

The holiday season approached, once again a mixture of joy and a nagging remorse for the perpetual incompleteness of the family unit. On Christmas morning they all went out to the graves and a heavy silence acknowledged a past never to be forgotten. The babies and Eve added a bolstered enjoyment of the festivities, and even Adagio received a new chew toy from Santa.

The winter months slipped by. Some mild spells allowed extended outings for the able dogs, and the family members often walked together with the dogs before engaging in a musical diversion.

The trend of the children gradually leaving the farm continued when Mandy left. Greg had a young lawyer friend in Boone, Peter Noble, who was starting his own practice and was in need of a legal secretary. Mandy's background was a natural connection, and they hit it off immediately upon an introduction and she agreed to work for him. She took a temporary furnished rental near to the office. A college town does have an ample assortment of rentals. One that was already furnished and pet friendly suited her well so she could bring Dramby with her. She was able to go to the apartment several times a day to check on her beloved canine friend and to change the piddle pad, although Dramby luxuriated most of the day in the massive plush dog bed that Mandy had gotten for the cherished pooch. Mandy and Peter started dating, and not a soul doubted that a romance was in the offing.

Ricky and Jean returned to Atlanta. The former ties there enticed them back with attractive monetary offers. There would be no financial strain to hire a nanny for John-John. None in the family wanted to hold them back so there was earnest encouragement for them to follow their plans. Ricky finally agreed to go after the mothers promised that with the diminishing family assistance they would hire help at the farm if all proved too daunting.

The most interesting development was a date that Wendy had. She met a fellow at the Library, and he seemed quite interested in her. She was luke warm about him although she could not put her finger on exactly what about him disturbed her. She reluctantly accepted his dinner invitation mainly because Candy encouraged her to try it out. It turned out to be a disappointment. Wendy knew it was wrong, but she could not help but compare him to Freeman and the newcomer fell far short in all categories. Memories may not always be as realistic as they should be, although they are difficult to alter. Wendy just knew that she would be unable to settle for any man who did not come close to what she once had. She vowed not to accept any more dates unless the prospect was compelling no matter how much Candy pressured her.

Adam, Helene, Eve, and Gordon were all who remained from the family's offspring nucleus. As the ladies sat on the bench early one chilly spring morning they had a sense that some opportunity would beckon this young family grouping to other vistas.

"Well, dear sisters of my heart, we suspected we would arrive at this point." Regina's voice was wistful. "We have gone full circle. I recall that long ago we had an extended talk about dreams. Now that we are getting on in years, it appears more difficult to determine where dreams end and reality begins."

"Or, where reality ends and dreams begin," Candy interrupted.

"Or, whatever," Wendy added. "Dreams or reality have to be lived, and taken one moment at a time. When we were young, I was confident we could control our future. Now I know that there are too many factors involved for us to control the future, and maybe even to some extent the future controls us. I am not even sure the present is as it seems to be. Each action and reaction can have variations and be subject to multiple interpretations. Even the past loses its confirmation as certain memories loom larger and clearer than others. The memories are colored by when or how we look back on them, and perhaps even why we look back on them."

"And, the most important thing," Regina interjected, "Is that living our own lives is difficult enough so we dare not try to live the lives of others, no matter how much we love and care about them. We'll miss the children and the grandchildren. Yet, their pathways are for their crossing. They'll be here for the meaningful times and holidays, and we need to make the most of that. I have no doubt if we should need them for more they'll be here for us as they know we are here for them. That is the essence of a family. You cannot make it and you cannot force it, but it is ours. Old age becomes clear in its design of a combination of letting go and giving up."

They stood up and headed back to the house arm-in-arm. Adagio scampered ahead knowing that when they reached the kitchen he would get one

of his special treats. Perhaps, dogs have the real secret to a contented life. What
is immediate is the true expectancy.

> *Where dwells the past? The pilgrim years,*
>> *The friends and hopes that we have known,*
>> *The timid smiles that swift have flown,*
> *Though swift, bedewed with bitter tears.*
>
> *Perchance on some great orb of space*
>> *The years and hopes and friends again*
>> *Live in the fleeting lives of men,*
> *The smiles and tears leave second trace.*

Revealed
John H. Stahl

Echo in the Heart

* * *

Fifteen

A bountiful spring cloaked the mountains with an array of colorful flowers and a proliferation of green buds. A fragrance of fresh sweetness hung in the air. It was amidst this glorious profusion that they gathered to discuss Dan's book *Not Lost — Just Not Found*.

Dan was forewarned that Ricky and Jean would not be there. Felicia and Greg came over along with Mandy and Peter. Peter had read Mandy's copy of the book.

Before the discussion got underway, Dan met briefly with the mothers. He sat them down and told them that he started a book about their lives as they wanted him to do. No doubt it would be an enjoyable undertaking for him. It was Wendy who inquired on behalf of them all. "How are you going to handle an ending?"

"Good question."

"I thought you would like it, Danzy."

"How would you handle this? When I have reached the final chapter, I'll let you read the draft of the book to that point. Then, and this should prove interesting for you, me, and the reader, you all write a final chapter as you see your life turning out and I will also write a final chapter. There will be two ending chapters.....an insider's version and an outsider's view."

"We'll have to think about that," Regina said guardedly.

"I expect nothing less."

With all gathered in the den, Dan looked around at the intent faces. "Well, don't all shout at once."

"I'll start," Candy spoke up enthusiastically. "I liked it. What intrigued me the most was how you made all of his patients such real people with honest issues even though there were just snippets of their problems."

Helene joined in. "As I was getting near the end and I saw there were not too many pages left, I wondered how you were going to end it. I probably should have seen it coming as you laid the framework leading into it, but I didn't. Once again, you did good, Danzy. And, once again, an amazingly different book from what has come before and I assume what will come after it."

Peter cleared his throat before speaking. "I certainly look forward to catching up on the books I have already missed. You have a knack of getting into the minds of your characters. Thoughts and value judgments interact, and it makes the reader want more. It does lead one to wonder how they all end up down the road. As a lawyer, I seek resolution, but an author can let the reader speculate about where or how a character will wind up. Very crafty of you, and I applaud the effort."

Opening her book, Felicia spoke next. "There were some great outlets for your ideas. I especially liked this part......

> *People erroneously think that the past, the present, and the future are separate and independent. Actually, they are intertwined. They are building blocks erecting the composite of who the person was, is, and will be. Not really three distinct persons but basically one and the same. This is such a difficult concept for young people to grasp."*

Helene nodded in agreement. "I thought the sayings at the end of each chapter were not only relevant to the story but also quite profound. Sure makes one think, and with so many of the things we do mechanically these days, it is a blessing to exercise the mind."

"I agree about the characters," Wendy edged her words in cautiously. "They not only came across as real, they were quite interesting. I particularly liked how they interacted whether it was by accident or design. The book could lead to a sequel, hey?"

Dan raised an eyebrow. "You are right, although frankly I hadn't thought of doing one for this book. Many clamber for a follow-up for *Network of Death*. I probably would do that one first, if ever. Here, the host of characters does have much of their lives ahead of them so it would probably not be a hardship to do a sequel. Fodder for thought."

Adam had to add his two cents. "I liked this part." He opened his book to a book marked site.

People are complex and simple at the same time.
Some are more of this, and some are less of that.
Each of us is different, and just that difference
can be a major asset. Our place in the scheme
of things is what we basically make of it on our
own. . . . One secret is not to look over your
shoulder to see where you have been. Look
ahead to a point you would like to be at. Pride
and satisfaction in that journey can bring your
own happiness. That is the cornerstone of a
sustainable life.

Candy opened her book. "This caught my fancy —

One of the greatest mysteries and challenges
of life is when an unanticipated development
stops you dead in your tracks. It can pull
the rug out from under your feet leaving you
unsettled in the clear path you thought you
were taking. There would be no way of
knowing whether you might land head or
feet first. Your direction can be intrepidly
changed.

We have experienced this. Our direction was changed, and to this day I am not sure whether we landed head or feet first."

"Did you study psychology?", Greg asked.

"I had a couple of courses in college, many moons ago. What I did here was an attempt to do what a psychologist might do to lead them to their own solutions."

Candy yelled out, "What's the next book, Danzy?"

"I do introduce each book to you as being different from the others. There will be no doubt in your minds with *Restless Beauty*. It is a mystery, not a murder mystery, but a mystery involving a lake that is deemed to have a restless spirit. It also has a host of varied characters, and I hope you will find it engrossing."

   After Dan signed the new book and went on his way back to his own log home high in the mountains, Wendy and Candy turned to Regina. Wendy spoke for them all. "How can we write an ending we have not lived yet?"

A certain sadness claims these autumn days —
   A sadness sweeter to the poet's heart
Than all the full-fed joys and lavish rays
   Of riper suns; old wounds, old woes depart;
Life calls a truce, and Nature seems to keep
Herself a-hush to watch the world asleep.

In the Fall
Alice R. Mylene

Sixteen

While the mothers watched Eve and Gordon, Adam and Helene walked down the lane and sat on the bench on the way back. The fresh greenery of the spring was restful to the eyes, and the air carried the sweet nectar smell of newly blossomed flowers.

Adam reached for Helene's hand and fingers intertwined. "Life is full of decisions, isn't it?"

The pressure of her fingers preceded her answer. "Dearest, there is no escaping it. I know this is a hard decision for you, and for me as well since I love it here and I love the mothers. They are mothers to me as well. Eve will be devastated leaving here as she thrives on all of this love. Gordon is just getting a taste of it. Whatever you decide, I support you as I always have and always will."

"I know that, and in a way it makes the decision more difficult." He was silent for a moment. "I suppose we will always wonder what this opportunity represents if we don't give it a chance. The one thing we have learned so well is that nothing is set in cement. We are always welcome here. If things don't work out, we'll just come back."

"Or, go on to other enticing opportunities if they open up."

"Yes. In a way, it is reassuring, maybe even exciting, to have options. As long as we are together, we'll just have to consider it all as an ongoing adventure."

"Perhaps we are just pioneers at heart."

"And in spirit."

Back at the house, they sat the mothers down in the den and told them of the decision to pursue an opportunity in Boston. They would leave just as soon as the mothers hired enough help for the dogs and the farm.

Candy, the birth mother, was the first to react. "Believe it or not, we sort of expected this sooner or later. We are the last ones to hold you back, you know that. Long ago we learned that dreams need to be pursued to quiet seething desires. We will miss you terribly, and if I were to joke about it we would keep Eve and Gordon as security. You are a loving family unit, and we just know you will make the most of your chances and each success will be a fortunate reflection on us."

Helene interjected, "We assure you we will be back for all of the family occasions. We are not leaving you. We are just branching out."

It was easier than they thought to get help. An increasing unemployment rate in the country afforded an easy vehicle to get farm help. Valarie had become so attached to the dogs that she readily agreed to work nearly a full schedule with the animals. She more than once wished she could take them all home with her.

Sarah Banes, who had answered the advertisement for shelter assistants, had been let go from her job at a downsized veterinarian's office, and she was a logical choice for an additional hand at the shelter. So, while it was not quite the same as having family, the mothers should not be burdened in their efforts.

It was a tearful departure when the group left for Boston. Talking it over beforehand, the mothers let Eve take Adagio with her. That togetherness was firmly entrenched and eased the good-byes. Attachments can work their own magic.

In the quiet that followed as the car drove away, the women went to the bench to tell the husbands of these recent developments. Holding hands, as they had done so often over the years, once again they could acknowledge the power of their togetherness. It had cushioned all of the upheavals and enhanced all of the meaningful moments. Regina once again likened it to the scope and depth of an echo in the heart.

"Another new chapter for the dream sisters," Wendy began. "And, it still does not make it any easier for me to think about writing a final chapter to our lives. How many chapters will there eventually be between this one and that one?"

"Makes one wonder," Regina offered.

"What choice do we have but to live each chapter as they come along? Our life story is our book. Each chapter is significant, I might even say powerful. It will be interesting to see if Dan can capture all of that essence in writing even if we can't." Having said this, Candy drew quiet, a wistful look fleeting across her face as she stared at Archer's grave.

They sat in silence as thoughts spiraled through the ups and downs of times gone by and an uncertain future beckoning them to proceed. The absence of the children and Adagio added to the pensiveness of the moment. Chirping spring birds served as the background music.

They returned to the home and tended to the dogs. After lunch they picked up their instruments and played the melodies they knew would soothe all agitation. The notes were words making their united stance against all adversities paramount.

I learn this lesson, O wood-path gray,
And trust its truths I may ne'er forget:
Each life must follow the self-same way
Of all who have smiled and sorrowed yet.

Do we reach the heights sublime and grand,
We press the foot-prints of others here;
Are we lost in the depths of "shadow-land."
The path is beaten; we need not fear.

Through Winding Ways
C. A. Neidig

Echo in the Heart

* * *

Seventeen

The following week Dan and Valarie came over for dinner, joined by Felcia, Greg, Mandy and Peter. It took three boxes of pasta and three loaves of garlic bread to complete the spaghetti meal that put them in a totally relaxed state to talk about Dan's book, *Restless Beauty*.

Once settled in the den, Dan did not have to prompt the discussion. Mandy was bursting at the seams and spoke right up. "Once again, writer man, the master storyteller has succeeded in producing a book totally different from the others. That really is an accomplishment."

Felicia quickly followed up on her sister's comments. "An engrossing story, too. A whole cast of interesting characters that you ingeniously used to tell a crafty story. I just marvel at how you develop each character just to the extent necessary to serve his or her role in the story, and then to keep the story moving along. Bravo, Danzy!"

"Sort of makes me want to see this lake," Peter pronounced. "I know it really doesn't exist, but in addition to the characters you did give it a life."

"Thanks," Dan related.

Mandy continued where she had left off. "A nice combination of drama, intrigue, and romance. All of your books are my favorites, but this one totally pleased my reading palate. A little scant on the usual proverbs, but I sure liked this line:

> *The young are impatient for love; older people are*
> *desperate once they get a taste of it."*

"And I liked this one for obvious reasons," Wendy exclaimed as she opened her book to the designated page:

> *Life is very fragile. The separation between life and*
> *death can be a matter of inches or seconds or degrees.*

"My favorite character is Christine," Regina spoke slowly. "Maybe, I am just at the age when I can identify with a life of one thing or another and yearning for something new. Don't get me wrong, I am content with my life and surroundings, but I can readily see and feel how it happens. She needed painting as a release just as I have had music to capture and release my pent-up spirit. I guess what I am trying to say is that I appreciate her as a real person, stymied in love and in a sense of fulfillment. What I would describe as a very human portrait. I am satisfied for her that she found what she so needed before it was too late."

Candy joined in. "Ginny, now that is a depressing note from the one of us who is always emotionally steadfast. The beauty of all of your books, Dan, is that the reader can surely identify closely with one or more of the characters. I think the most uplifting aspect of the book is that each person, other than the evil brothers, found the element missing from their lives. By the way, was it one of the brothers that struck Gail on the head?"

"Ah," Dan grinned. "That is the puzzle for the reader to unravel. It could have been one of the brothers, or one of the Indian descendants, or a disgruntled construction worker, present or past, or one of the fishermen ghosts. Perhaps, other remote possibilities can surface when you delve into it. Who do you think it was?"

"One of the brothers, for sure. They resented her intrusion, and they probably wanted to scare her off. Economic disaster can prompt violence and other tragic acts."

"Sounds plausible."

Does Love bring peace? Aye, more, a glad rejoicing,
Happier by far than song of merry bird;
In language of its own it finds a voicing,
Sweeter than any speech the ear hath heard,
Clearer than spoken word.

Can Love endure? Aye, ceaseless as the ocean,
Firm as a rock o'er which mad billows break;
There is no limit to its deep devotion,

No sacrifice too great for one to make
For its dear, cherished sake.

Does Love change? Aye, the scented breath of summer,
Whispering low to blossoming flowers entwined,
Is not more faithless than this fair new comer;
But oh, unlike the sighing, swaying wind,
Love leaves a trace behind.

Does Love die? Aye,—then lo! at night uprisen,
A wan and vengeful spirit slips its chain
And cheats us to our rest. Forsakes its prison
To glide into our dreams, and wake the pain
We thought forever slain.

Love
Lillian Plunkett

Echo in the Heart

* * *

Eighteen

It was only the mothers in attendance at the discussion of Dan's latest novel, *Glimpses of Forgotten Dreams*. Perhaps, that was most appropriate since the book revolves around the lives of some very special elderly people. Felicia and Mandy were involved with other distractions with Greg and Peter, although they all had read the book and conveyed their accolades.

Dan and Valarie had dinner with the ladies, and after cleaning up from the sumptuous meal, they gravitated to the den and made themselves comfortable on the oversized sofa and chairs. With Adagio now Eve's dog, the ladies had missed a dog's close presence in their relaxing moments. They had selected a female yorkie mix from the shelter brood, a dog they named Lento, who was about five years old and had been greatly mistreated before arrival at the shelter. Lento had burn scars across her belly and was blinded in one eye, apparently by some sharp object. Yet, she had exhibited in a remarkable short period of time a capacity for docile affection and an intelligent response to gentle commands and loving hands. She quickly adapted to having freedom to roam the house but followed the ladies wherever they went. She was enthralled by their music, and it further soothed her mannerism. Her greatest pleasure was curling up in any lap that was offered to her.

Once settled, Regina initiated the discussion. "I am simply and constantly amazed how each of your books is different, each distinct in its own way. While equally enthralling, each one seems better than the previous one. I shed a tear now and then in several of your books, but in this one I literally cried me a river. You show great empathy for old people. I will welcome entering my old age if only I can be cared for by such fine people portrayed in the story. I guess what I am trying to say, and probably not too well, is that this book should be required reading for young and old alike. It would be eye opening for youngsters to realize that old people have dreams and deep feelings, and it can comfort those who have reached the winter of their lives that dreams can be remembered and the joys of living are never too late to grasp. It is insightful all around."

"Well put," Candy added. "I just loved the story and felt extremely close to the characters. You made them come alive. They are so real. Your treatment of dying is tasteful and thought provoking. It sure carries a powerful message, and I agree with Ginny that everyone could learn much from the book."

"Very kind words, ladies." Dan smiled broadly and grasped Valarie's hand. "I can't tell you how rewarding it is for an author to know that his thoughts register with the readers and are so well received."

Regina spoke up again. "It is a book that will stay with us for many years to come. We have read many of the great books of the past, and yours can stand proud with the whole gamut of them. I look forward to reading it again, I dare say many times, and I just know I will find new wisdom and pleasure in each reading. I like to think of it raising a new harvest of emotions. If I may, this was one of my favorite parts, when you describe the plight of so many residents in a retirement home.

> Lives are compartmentalized, and as soon as the new aspect
> of a life is entered where apparent uselessness seems
> pervasive, body and mind are cast aside to wither and die.
> Being provided for is surely an empty gesture when
> unaccompanied by love, respect and compassion. No less a
> person because of age and infirmity, the elderly are forced
> to exist in that preordained mode until death becomes a
> welcome relief. Old mouths can speak but young ears do
> not want to listen. Society turns its back on a valuable asset,
> those who are tried and true.

In fact, this also is forever etched in my heart along with the echo that resides there. Yes, old folks can know the pleasure of love. Stanley and Lauren have shown the world.

> They lay upon the bed and his arms enfolded her. He bent
> over and sealed their magical moment with a kiss. Young
> lips do have a certain sweetness. Old lips, even when
> parched and cracked, have a beguiling nectar. It is the
> taste of a confirmation of living, the unshakeable belief
> that only death can deprive the heart of its beat and the

*emotions it can engender. The splendor of love was
revealed to have no bounds, no age. They entered a calm
sleep. Dying bodies can share new life."*

Candy opened her copy of the book. "This was full of significance for me and what we have had in our lives.

A lifetime can be in a moment.

Adding to Ginny's enchantment with your description of love elders can feel, I was very much taken by Dora and Tucker's hold on a flash of love.

*The future was a day at a time. Dreams were short-term
and still vivid, and no less poignant than those of young
lovers who believe the world is theirs forever. An old
love is special because it holds no rash promises of
extreme pleasures or outlandish results. It focuses on
the here and now."*

"And I have to accentuate my favorite part," Wendy offered quietly.

*"Dora calmly exclaimed that she was not afraid to die.
Accepting death is not any different than taking other
things in stride. Life can have many twists and turns,
and the secret to not letting them derail you is to meet
them on their own terms. Death is final only if one
deems it to be.*

As you know, when we lost our husbands, we lost part of our lives. It is the death of those that we love that is harder to bear than thinking of our own death. I suppose we will expound on this in the writing of the last chapter. You, however, have gotten us to thinking about it. And as long as we are on a sad note, I am forlorn in knowing that there are no more Danzy books to read."

"I am well into the book about the dream sisters. As long as you agreed to the writing of your final chapter, how far into it are you?"

"We have discussed it at length," Candy responded. "We have even made some notes. It is a challenging endeavor for sure, almost scary to try and put the future down in writing. Yet, when you are ready for it I dare say it will fall into place. That is if we can agree among ourselves. It sure will be interesting to see if our ending or yours will closely match what will be."

> *There is but one way into life, but death*
> *   Comes in a thousand ways, a thousand forms,*
> *   Its voice is heard within the howling storms,*
> *Its touch is felt in the hot fever's breath.*

"When Wouldst Thou Die?"
F. P. Kopta

Nineteen

It was a sunny and warm summer day, quite inappropriate for the pending occasion. Felicia was driving and Mandy sat pensively in the passenger's seat as they made the twenty-five minute drive from Boone to the farm. They would be the only representatives of the children at the marking of the third anniversary of the deaths of the fathers.

They talked every day, often for a long time. Sisters who are close seem to have a variety and abundance of topics and points to convey and discuss. The projection of the day's events lent a serious note to the talking.

Mandy looked at Felicia's finely etched profile and once again thought she was by far the prettier and more robust sister. "We are at a crossroads, don't you think?"

"Yes. Some tough choices lay ahead. What will you do if Peter asks you to marry him?"

"I'm not sure. He is a good man, but I just feel that something is lacking. I can't put my finger on it. He has not warmed up to Dramby as I had hoped he would. We know through our own childhood with the dogs and now with the shelter that the way a person reacts with and to animals is a telltale sign of the depth of sensitivity. Being so sensitive myself, I would not ever be truly comfortable with someone who does not match or exceed my feelings. He is not as affectionate as I would hope either. We grew up in such an affectionate environment. I want and need that always."

"Funny, I feel the same way about Greg."

"If Peter asks me to live with him, it might be a chance to really get to know him intimately, but I don't want it to be interpreted as any form of commitment. I probably would say no to such an arrangement. There is little to be gained by entering a road that you suspect travels nowhere. I sure wish *Poppa* were still here. He had a real knack for cutting through the fluff and pinpointing what is involved."

"Yes, he was a master at clear thinking and giving relevant advice. I could sure use him as a sounding board about Greg too. It is comforting having him around all of the time. Yet, something is missing. Maybe, it is a kind of generation gap of some sort. Our points of reference are in two different time periods. He is consumed by his painting. It is the true love of his life, and I just don't see him sharing that with a person. While music and reading saturate my being, I believe I have room for a love interest with a person and the outgrowth of those feelings. I would also like to have a child before my biological clock winds all the way down. We have never really talked about it, but I am sure he would find that an intrusion and a distraction from his painting. *Poppa* often told us that we should measure life's goals by what is important and worthwhile. I just don't see the compatibility of that scenario with Greg. I am not even sure if I was not there that he would miss me."

"*Poppa* undoubtedly would counsel both of us to give ourselves as much time as we needed to be sure about things. Our minds and hearts will eventually settle the matter. We should not give ourselves any undue pressure. Although if I hear our words right there seems to be a troubling future. Speaking about a troubling future, what about the mothers?"

"That is starting to be a major concern, isn't it?"

"Yes. I hate leaving them alone with so much to do and under such emotional strain."

"You don't think that Valarie and Sarah are enough help?"

"For the physical aspects, probably so. It is not the same as being surrounded by family, especially our loving family. Nothing is stronger than that. We learn that lesson repeatedly. Frankly, I see them growing tired and old before my eyes, and it alarms me. I can identify my own frailness with their aging. I am afraid for me at times, and now scared for them all of the time. Three overwhelming questions come to my mind. Who will take care of them? Who will look out after me? And, what will happen to the farm and the shelter?"

"Dearest, Mandy," Felicia uttered in nearly a whisper as she reached for her sister's hand. "I promise you that I will always be here for and with you. As for our mothers, you have always been so sensitive as to see danger signs long before anyone else does. Whenever you think a crisis is looming ahead, we'll call a Children's Council as we used to do when we were all young and a collective decision had to be made or a subject talked out. I had almost forgotten what a vital part of our growing years that action was until I told Dan about it when we were talking about our growing up in a commune so that he would have some further matters to put in the book. I realize how important that is. It was the first thing I revealed to him after boasting about the benefits of having multiple parents. That sort of security blanket runs from old to young and young to old." She hesitated for an instant. "As for the farm, I shudder to think it might no longer be. We spent our entire lives there. It is our growing up place, our refuge. It is probably another bridge we have to cross when we get there, and it will not be an easy thing."

They pulled into the farm and were quickly greeted with warm embraces from the mothers. They went into the kitchen to partake of a Caesar salad lunch at the picnic table. After relaxing for a time and further catching up on recent developments, they headed out to the graves. Mandy's touch with animals made a big impression on Lento. She tagged along at her feet as they walked.

The plan was for each to have selected a poem to be read aloud after a period of silent meditation. They held hands, and the echo in the heart was strong and clear.

Felicia read a poem by Vachel Lindsay;

> *Sleep softly . . . eagle forgotten . . .*
> > *under the stone,*
> *Time has its way with you there and*
> > *the clay has its own.*
> *Sleep on, O brave-hearted, O wise man,*
> > *that kindled the flame —*
> *To live in mankind is far more than to*
> > *live in a name.*

Mandy read this by Emily Dickinson:

> *On this wondrous sea,*
> > *Sailing silently,*
> *Ho! pilot, ho!*
> *Knowest thou the shore*
> *Where no breakers roar,*
> > *Where the storm is o'er?*

In the silent west
Many sails at rest,
>*Their anchors fast;*
Thither I pilot thee, —
Land, ho! Eternity!
>*Ashore at last!*

Pulling out a sheet of paper tucked in her pocket, Regina read this poem by Hans Zinsser:

>*How sweet the Summer! And the*
>>*Autumn shone*
>*Like warmth within our hearts as in the*
>>*sky,*
>*Ripening rich harvests that our love*
>>*had sown,*
>*How good that ere the Winter comes, I*
>>*die!*
>*Then, ageless in your heart, I'll come to*
>>*rest*
>*Serene and proud, as when you loved*
>>*me best.*

Candy pulled open a book she was carrying on the writings of Edgar Allan Poe, and she sobbed as she read the following:

>*Thou wast all that to me, love,*
>>*For which my soul did pine:*
>*A green isle in the sea, love,*
>>*A fountain and a shrine*
>*All wreathed with fairy fruits and flowers,*
>>*And all the flowers were mine.*

Ah, dream too bright to last!
> *Ah, starry Hope, that did arise*
But to be overcast! . . .
> *my spirit hovering lies*
Mute, motionless, aghast.

For alas! alas! with me
> *The light of Life is o'er!*
> *No more—no more—no more—*
>> *. . .*
Shall bloom the thunder-blasted tree,
> *Or the stricken eagle soar.*

And all my days are trances,
> *And all my nightly dreams*
Are where thy gray eye glances,
> *And where they footstep gleams—*
In what ethereal dances,
> *By what eternal streams.*

Wendy read a couple of stanzas from a favorite poem by Henry Wadsworth Longfellow:

And forever and forever,
> *As long as the river flows,*
As long as the heart has passions,
> *As long as life has woes;*

The moon and its broken reflection
> *And its shadows shall appear,*
As the symbol of love in heaven,
> *And its wavering image here.*

They lingered for a spell feeling the warmth of the day spread over them and to know that their love for one another can carry to the grave. Interestingly, as they had talked about it many times, they for sure thought that throughout their lives there would be secrets that they had to harbor. As it turned out there never were any secrets. All was open and there never was a need for hidden confidences. That also was a tribute to a remarkable friendship.

> *O hope's, fair roses, that once were blooming*
> > *With fragrance sweet in my throbbing breast,*
> *I long to see you again returning*
> > *To life, and soon give my heart sweet rest.*
> *Come back to me and forever stay!*
> *Bid all my sorrows pass far away!*

One Morning in the Garden
Isidorus

Twenty

An exceptionally early frost came to the valleys, and according to the locals such portends a harsh winter ahead. The other telltale signs confirming that theory were an abundance of wooly bears, the deer turning dark early, and a bumper crop of acorns.

The women had reviewed Dan's draft of the book of their lives. It appropriately is entitled *Echo in the Heart*. They tried to maximize their time and efforts towards writing their version of the final chapter. Soon, the Christmas tree harvesting would occupy whatever free time they now enjoyed after tending to the demands of the shelter. Musical ensembles had become by necessity trios at resort functions, and even that would have to be put on hold until the Christmas tree endeavor wound down.

"Reading about our lives sure seems full and satisfying," Candy uttered as they were in the kitchen one morning lingering over a second cup of coffee. "Sort of parallels drinking this second cup of coffee, a ritual that I look forward to each morning. It is the last vestige of the night's rest, and is a gentle transition to our hectic day."

Regina looked up from filling Lento's water bowl. She returned to sipping the dark liquid. The three of them had always drunk coffee black. "If we did not lose our men and all of our parents early, I don't think there would be any other truly down moments we could point to."

"I have always felt bad," Wendy said in a hushed and melancholy tone, "About not having a really close relationship with our parents. They did eventually accept our way of marrying and living, but it could have been so much more. I resolve to be the best grandparent possible and, hopefully, a constant presence in our grandchildren's lives. A proverbially strong and scenic bridge across generations."

Candy looked out of the window studying how the frost adhered to each blade of grass. "There is little sense brooding over a past that cannot be changed."

Regina placed her now empty cup in the sink. "Even the in-laws are gone. Perhaps, the kindest act of all concerning them is that none of them were still alive to see the death of their sons."

"Short life genes for us and the children," Wendy spoke hesitatingly. "That is why we must face the issue of our deaths in the chapter. And, we need to tackle it directly. I want to be the first to go so I do not have to deal with losing either of you."

"Smart talk," Regina exclaimed. "We'll deal with it because we have to. As with the men, we will concentrate on what we had and not on what we lost. What I don't think I can handle is if any of the children should die before me. We have already lost two dogs in the shelter recently, and even that has been difficult. All creatures need to live reasonably long lives."

Wendy placed a hand on Regina's arm. "I shudder even to think of such an eventuality. I don't want to think about it, and certainly we should not include anything like that in the chapter."

"Oh, no," Regina grimaced. "It will be our ending and no one else's."

"Let's end this depressing discussion, please," Candy exhorted. "No matter how we may write about it, we will all die either in our sleep on the same night or we will all have a heart attack while playing a Hungarian Rhapsody."

The chuckles lightened the air and calmed the moment. Yet, the matter would not be fully at rest. It was tempting to tell Dan to just do an ending chapter without any input from them. However, they could and should not avoid telling about a closing to their lives, so they might just as well put it down on paper.

Like the spring warms into summer,
　　Bursting bud to flowering plume,
And the hardy orchard blossom
　　Bears an apple in its womb;
So the mind expands and strengthens,
　　Seeing with its practiced eye
How to weave the web of fancy
　　And the filament supply,
How to voice its ripe perceptions
　　That the wrath of time defy.

While the fog o'er hangs the ocean,
*   Ships bewildered ride the foam,*
When it lifts they find their bearings
*   And the breezes speed them home;*
So from mists of doubtful seeming
*   Mind will languish to be free,*
Only as its insight clears up
*   Can its outlook 'cross the sea*
Fill the soul with inspiration
*   To attain its destiny.*

Looking Outward
T. Park Bucher

Echo in the Heart

* * *

Twenty-One

Helene glanced around the small and sterile Boston townhouse, and it stifled her enthusiasm. Eve was playing on the floor with Adagio, and John-John was in the playpen enthralled by the musical mobile. She had just kissed Adam good-bye as he left for work, and knew he was not comfortable having to wear a suit and tie.

Looking out of the front window at all of the cement, the cars, and the similar houses bunched together, a longing for the vistas and naturalness of the farm took hold of her mood. Gazing out the back window fared no better. A solid high wood fence enclosed the postage-stamp sized yard, barely big enough for Eve to run in circles with the dog. No free spaces to romp and roam. As she sipped the remaining coffee in her cup, the thought resonated to her core that while being together is the best thing, where you are together might be just as important.

It hung heavy on her mind all day. Even the walk with Eve, Adagio, and John-John in the stroller did little to soothe the anxiety. The noise of the city, including blaring horns and heavy truck traffic, sent her mind only to focus on the place where her soul was at peace and where she saw Adam relaxed and smiling, and the environment where Eve was unrestrained and unabashed.

Back in the townhouse, she played on the spinet they had gotten on a monthly rental from the music shop at the mall. That just seemed to accentuate the restlessness of her spirit.

She telephoned the mothers, and while that was comforting for the moment, it was not the same as conversing in person. Eve was animated speaking to them, but she was glum after they hung up. "When are we going home?" That is the way Eve phrased it, and that just about summed it up.

The children were put to bed early after dinner. Helene and Adam lingered at the small kitchen table. She reached across for his hand and clutched at his fingers. "The only good news today is that I did get my first piano student. Otherwise, the day was filled with letdowns. At the supermarket, I shuddered at the temptingless condition of the produce. What I would give for a *Moon Music Farm* succulent apple or a juicy white peach. The noise, the pollution, and the struggle between nature and man where nature has been victimized, sure is depressing. Adam, my dear Adam, the children and I miss the serenity, we miss the opportunity to run carefree through the orchards and the Christmas trees. We miss the mothers. We talked to them on the telephone, and it actually made it worse because it tasted like more. Eve asked when we are going home. Need I say more?"

Adam covered her hand with his. "You have said it all, my sweet. You know I feel the same way, and I would much rather the children grow up in the kind of environment I had as a boy. I groan each time I have to put on a suit and tie, as you know. The job is mechanical, and not at all challenging. Yet, the money is good, and there is a certain amount of security in getting a regular paycheck."

"I do know you are torn between what you think we need and what we want. I assure you the money does not outweigh the negatives of city living."

Adam raised an eyebrow, and his voice was as stern as she had ever heard it. "We took the big step, and it is a drastic change. I am the first one to admit that. But, we need to give it a chance so that we can confirm what is best for all of us. We'll be revitalized with our visits on Thanksgiving and Christmas. There is a year's lease on this place and, fortunately, we did not take all of our furniture here, just the basic stuff. Let's see the year out, and if the negatives are still present, we'll know what we have to do. We will also know that with certainty and finality."

Helene bent her head down and kissed the back of his hand. "It is exasperating at times that you are so damned reasonable. I know that is right. Maybe, it's best, and it makes sense. I just foresee this being a long and dismal year. I'd even bet what will be the decision then. If Eve did not have Adagio, she would be completely miserable. If I did not have the piano to lose myself in, I might not make it. I wish I were as strong as you."

"And I wish I were as strong as you. I may not have told you often enough, you are the bedrock of this family. Your gentleness and loving spirit guides us all. Little wonder our little family and the larger one are all crazy about you, especially me."

"You give me much too much credit. My expanded heart is my only strength."

"That proves my point. That, dear, is tremendous power."

They embraced and kissed tenderly, a kiss engendering the warmth

and vitality of deep emotions and the majesty of broad human capabilities. A
tomorrow together is a secure and sane future.

> *On the clean white sand I traced a name*
> > *And watched the waves as they washed it out,*
> *And tho't in life it was just the same—*
> *That you lived and died with sands washed white.*
> *I cut a name in a white birch tree,*
> *'Twas youth's wild folly that made me do,*
> *But heart and sense will both agree*
> *That bark will cover the cut anew.*
>
> *I cut with love a name in my heart,*
> *Patiently traced the letters there,*
> *But the tide of passion formed a part,*
> *An inevitable ending in despair.*
> *I cut a name in marble stone*
> *And the ivy crept and covered a grave;*
> *The wind thro' the trees but echo a moan,*
> *The best is lost in trying to save.*

Engraven
E. L. Macomb Bristol

Echo in the Heart

* * *

Twenty-Two

Nearly an exact replica was being played out in Atlanta. Returning to an old job was not quite the familiar friend as one might hope for. Ricky had almost forgotten how unpleasant it was to be involved in office politics. The stress filtering into the daily routine was a stark contrast to the worthwhile endeavors at the farm and dog shelter. The tug on his heartstrings was undeniable.

Jean felt uncomfortable with the thought of leaving the baby with a stranger. She decided to be a stay-at-home mom. The apartment they were renting was comfortable although quite cramped compared to the expansive space at the farm. The walls were not well soundproofed so voices and televisions from other units could be heard. Undoubtedly, many of the other tenants could hear Gordon when he cried. There was a park close by, and she spent a good part of nice days there with Gordon. Yet, it was crowded and she could not quite relax there. She talked with other mothers, and while pleasant there was just no intellectual stimulation as there had been at the farm, especially when talking about Dan's books. The tolerance for talk about children and shopping was wearing thin and contributed to a brooding discontent.

Ricky and Jean talked often about their present and future life. Each time they wound up at the same apparently final point. There could be no better life for them and for Gordon than at the farm.

It was too premature for any major action. It had been a big step to return to Atlanta and the consequences of that move were not yet fully known. If any major upheaval lay ahead, they wanted to make sure they were fully ready to carry them out. Meanwhile, they would look forward to the holidays at the farm with the family.

Developments with Felicia and Mandy in Boone were also substantial. Felicia's final acceptance that Greg could not forego enough of his artistic life for having a family led to the decision to terminate any close relationship. The break up was cordial. She moved in with Mandy as she had gotten a fabulous job in the Music Library at Appalachian State University. She could easily commute from the farm, but she wanted to live up to her words that she would be there for Mandy. Being with her would facilitate the keeping of that promise.

Mandy had become more and more disenchanted with Peter. She did not really blame him for not living up to her high expectations. Yet, once the disappointment set in, there was no way she could rationalize it away. They stopped seeing each other on a personal level and limited it to the business at the office. It was not the best of situations, but Mandy was going to give it more time to see if she might be wrong. Emotional certainty was the only way there would be no lingering regrets.

The sisters discussed at length whether to move back to the farm and commute together, or to stay in Boone for now. They decided to stay. Both knew too well that once back at the farm the pull to remain there and abandon the jobs would be strong. Felicia still harbored the desire to meet a man to love and to have a baby. It was a compartmentalized dream, and she did not want to close that door until she had to. Her job at the Library already had given her an opportunity to meet music lovers. That was mentally stimulating and promising. She might even meet someone for Mandy. Being a musician and brought up in a house filled with music and reading, a romantic was born and perpetuated.

Would you regret
If I no more should stand
Thy clasped hand
    In mine,
The while your sheltering arm
Safe shielded me from harm
    Would you regret
    That we had met?

Would you regret
If to the silent tomb
Strong arms should bear
    Me, hence;
Ah, dearest, would you miss
My warm impassioned kiss,

Would you regret
That we had met?

Would you regret
That you had weary been
With my shortcomings often
            Sorely tried,
Because forsooth one day
I claimed to have my way,
Your will defied
            Will you regret
            That we had met?

Would calm regret
Persuade you to the spot
Where I were lowly laid,
Would you bend low and shed
            A tear
Above me calmly sleeping there,
            The words you've said
            Would you regret,
Alas! That we had met.

Would You Regret
Josie D. Henderson-Heard

Echo in the Heart

* * *

Twenty-Three

With the labored final chapter in hand, the ladies went to Dan and Valarie's home for dinner. After a succulent meal of baked salmon with lemon and dill, they sat in the living room and exchanged writings.

Valarie was busy in the kitchen cleaning up from the feast. Dan read the women's chapter, and he had made three copies of his ending so each could read it at the same time.

"Wow!" Candy burst out with an emphatic exclamation after savoring each page. "Talk about totally different endings!"

"I'll say," Regina added. "There is probably room for a third ending somewhere between these two. Of course, Danzy, I like your ending better although I think ours is more realistic. It is in our power to plan it that way. If I could project myself into the future it would be quite interesting to see what really happens."

"Take me with you," Wendy gestured with her arms outstretched. "I love your ending, Zappo. It is the one we, of course, would cherish. Yet, it illustrates that too often sacrifice is required for meaningful deeds. I am not sure I am comfortable with that. I'll really have to think about it. Maybe, even cry over it as well. Imagine, a grown woman crying over something that hasn't happened yet and may not even come to pass."

"Does it really matter?" Dan's voice was earnest. "I am privileged to have written your wonderful story. I hope I captured the uniqueness of your lives and the warmth and caring of all who have been affected by your presence and values. I like your ending because it is as unselfish as the lives you have lived. No demands and no regrets for what you have done and are doing. Who else can say that? You have capped the special friendship logically and in the sort of significance that is relevant to you. I know readers will very much appreciate how you see the future for yourselves."

"Kind words, writer man." Wendy went to Dan and gave him three hugs. "That's from all of us. They'll do the same, I know. Somehow, you will have gotten nine hugs from three."

"I like the new math," Dan said grinning. "Hugs are the source of a writer's fountain of creativity, especially from three wonderful lasses. Valarie has read my ending, and I just know she will appreciate your chapter. The two are an engrossing counterpoint."

"So, where do we go from here?" Regina's look of puzzlement matched her inquiry. "The children will be surprised, I think, and they'll certainly have reactions to both endings with pointed comments."

Dan raised an eyebrow. "Good. The book club will be confronted with its utmost challenge. Just when they thought there were no more books, the one closest to them arrives. All four of us will have to sign their copies."

Regina continued with her author quiz. "Then, I gather, we do not let the children pass on the endings before the book is printed?"

"That's what I was thinking," Dan responded. "But, if you would rather them read it first that is alright with me."

Candy spoke up emphatically. "I know they would just respect what has been done, so my thought is just to let it ride. If we open it up for discussion, I dare say none of us will recognize the final result. This way, they can debate it as an after fact, which is mighty interesting in its own right. And, I want to be around when they talk about it. I can see it now, they'll want greater details, more intense expressions of thoughts, and a larger role for themselves as the players in the wings."

"Sounds about right to me," Wendy interposed.

"Then we are in agreement, my beloved counterparts." Regina went to Dan to give him her three hugs. "It is a feat complete."

Candy gave Dan her three hugs. "Sure is nice to hug a man. I hope Valarie is not the jealous type and will come running out from the kitchen to scratch my eyes out. We'll give her a hug too as she is a major part of who you are."

"She sure is!"

> Above the steps of stone so cold,
> Above the steps a tale is told
> Of life that would live because it must,
> Of life and growth in darkness and dust;
> For a green leaf smiled at the flow'rets fair,
> Showering their glory everywhere;

And more to me than the roses gold,
Was the wealth of praise one leaf could hold.
Ah, leaf as brave! how many there be
In human life, seeking light like thee!

Seeking the Light
Lester M. Houch

Echo in the Heart

* * *

Twenty-Four

THE FINAL CHAPTER WRITTEN BY
REGINA, CANDY, AND WENDY

They built a campfire. It was the campfire as at Camp Melody and they were young once again. As the fire blazed before them, they held hands anew. Together they shouted out, "Friends for life. Friends for all yesterdays and tomorrows." The intervening years inspired them to add to the oath: "Cherish the yesterdays; dream for the tomorrows." In the silence now there was just the reassuring pressure of the clasped hands to mark the culmination of the discussion they had labored through.

All now at the age of seventy-four, Candy who had repeatedly displayed the same enthusiastic attitude she had at the age of thirteen, was the first to offer her comments. "It makes so much darned sense that I am thinking it is way out of character for us. It calls to me, and I respond in the only way I know. We did good!"

Wendy quickly joined in. "What you really mean is that we have been sensible all of our lives so that now when we are near the end we should not make sense."

"It is, my dear sisters of the heart, a bit of both." Regina gazed into the fire, each flame representing an aspect of their lives, each flame ending in smoke disappearing into the darkness of the night. The light and warmth of the flame gone but the memory of each one lingering in the eye and mind of the watcher. "It is not what we may have hoped for, but it involves only us and raises no demands on others. The children are on their own pathways in a world that is already in turmoil. They must fend for themselves. They should not feel that our personal lives are a distraction that needs attention. That is probably the best thing we can do for them. We can help them by declaring that we do not need their help."

The tears flowed from Wendy's eyes. "I will miss this place. So much of us is here. I do not want to be far from Freeman."

"You know we can come here to visit whenever we want and are able to,"

Regina said softly as a tear rolled slowly down her cheek. "As each of us dies, we will be cremated as we have agreed upon, and our ashes will be spread on our husbands' graves. The farm and all that goes with it will be divided among the children and grandchildren when the last of us is gone. The lawyer clearly set this forth in our wills, with portions in trust for any grandchildren under age. Until that point, we will be together and that makes the most sense, even if it is just to us. That is our friendship for tomorrow and for whatever tomorrows remain for us."

Prompted throughout the years, the major concern repeatedly hashed out and decided upon was that they not be a burden to any of the children. Discovering the new and unique retirement home for musicians opening in Asheville, they went there for a briefing and tour. All phases of assisted living would be available along with musical facilities and opportunities of many varieties. After a third visit and detailed tour, they put a deposit down on a chalet that backed up to the woods. Medical and commercial needs were conveniently established on the grounds of the facility, along with open spaces, gardens, and walking paths. Housekeeping and dining would be included for all residents.

Valarie had eagerly agreed to be the full-time manager of the shelter, and Sarah and her husband would live in the house for as long as necessary to run and supervise the Christmas tree business, the scaled down farm activities, and assist Valarie with the dogs. The women and children could visit and stay at any time. The graves would be protected and perpetually cared for.

It was a rather simple arrangement to a potentially complex situation. If the children were unhappy with not being consulted, they would not be able to deny the practical attractiveness of the plan. The ladies knew if they opened the matter up for discussion, the children would argue about it among themselves without any firm and unanimous resolution.

They sat at the campfire until the last embers disappeared. They never let go of their hands.

Back at the house, they played many of their favorite musical pieces. The notes were sweet and the melodies lingered in a form of reassurance they were taking the right step. Over all of the years, the friendship had never failed them. It would not do so now or ever. The oath was sacrosanct. The echo in the heart had an infinite glow to it to light their way.

Twenty-Five

THE FINAL CHAPTER WRITTEN
BY THE AUTHOR

One might think that after a number of the shelter dogs dying, the ladies would be stoic about such a happening. As they emerged from the veterinarian's office after Lento was put to sleep, they took a moment to hug. In the car, before starting back to the farm, they sobbed to mark the departure of a special dog that shared so many times of togetherness. Just one more in a series of voids. Just one more aspect to dwell upon in the fragile vulnerability of life, both human and animal. One of the most difficult decisions to have to make is when is it time to put an end to suffering?

At the farm, they sat upon the bench. Wendy spoke slowly and softly. "Losing Lento just brings to the front burner the issue we need to face once and for all. Each of us now has medical problems which will progressively get worse. I scare myself each time I look in the mirror. I do not recognize the old lady I see there. I do not deny old age and accept the decline, even if not graciously. Yet, that is not enough. Our energy and attentiveness to the shelter and farm is already waning. I would like to think, dear sisters of my heart, some careful crafting for the rest of our lives is in order."

"What are the options?" Candy interposed with a hint of exasperation.

A few moments passed. Regina spoke up in a steady voice. "The way I see it, we have three choices. First, we can stay here and care for each other as long as we can. Second, we can call upon some or all of the children to be here as our caretakers. Or, third, we can go to a nursing home and be under professional care."

Wendy stood up and walked around the graves. Sitting back on the bench, her words came out nearly in a whisper. "We are already in the first option. That is our choice by desire and necessity."

"I agree," Candy uttered. "Where it goes from here, if it goes at all, we should probably leave it up to the children."

"What do you mean if it goes at all?" Wendy was determined in her question.

"We might get to a point where our care is beyond our choice."

"Oh."

Regina frowned. "Since we have no crystal ball, the only thing we can do is to tell the children what we are doing. Most likely, when it comes down to any tough decisions, they may have to make them with or without our input. We may be at a point where we cannot speak for ourselves."

"Strange," Wendy stated with emphasis, "I can't remember a time when we were not the ones to make the decisions. Even our men left decisions to us. Growing old, being infirm, and with a growing dependence on others, is for the birds."

"That's why there are vultures." Candy smiled broadly.

When the family was assembled for Christmas, the women expounded on what was on their minds concerning their future care. It was the time for a longer stay and presented more opportunity for discussion. There was some reluctance to dampen the Christmas spirit but with the family all together it was opportune.

Adam, as the eldest, called a gathering of the Children's Council. Since Helene and Jean were also affected and now considered loving children of the mothers, they were part of the Council proceedings.

Gathering in the den while the mothers were off in the bedrooms with the grandchildren, Adam called the Council to order. "We have not met like this for a long time, and the structure is just a formality. We know what the issue is, and I don't think we have to actually take a vote. It is just important that we speak our minds and our hearts and agree on what can and should be done. I do not have to recognize any of you to speak. Just do so as you are moved to do."

Felicia rose from the sofa. "Mandy and I have actually discussed this possibility a number of times recently as we have seen the decline in vigor and health of our mothers. Being here often, and driving them to the doctors and for tests, we have known that a time is near for us to move back to the farm and be the caretakers. We can also watch over the shelter with Valarie and Sarah's help, as well as keep the farm running even on a scaled back version. We have no husbands, no children, and there is no real reason in light of the developments here for us to stay in Boone. Our jobs cannot sway us to stay there under these circumstances, and we strongly feel our place is here. We assure you that the two of us can handle what confronts us, and if we cannot we would call for another Children's Council meeting."

Mandy nodded the entire time Felicia was speaking. They were of one mind, and there was no need for an additional pronouncement.

"That is all well and good, my loving sisters," Ricky's voice was slow-paced. "And, of course, it is nothing less than what we would expect of you both. I also have no doubt whatsoever that you both could handle it all most adequately. We would feel most confident our mothers would be receiving the best of attention. Yet, there is more at stake here. Jean and I not only want to be here to help and give you and the mothers our support, we want to be here period. Atlanta or anywhere else is not for us. We belong here, and this is where Gordon should be to grow up and flourish as nowhere else can hold a candle to this home. We were going to give it some more time before deciding to move back here for good, but this is the impetus for doing what we are gong to do anyway. It was just a matter of time."

It was Jean's turn to nod continuous approval of Ricky's words. She grasped his hand as a final gesture of agreement.

Adam beamed. "Talk about taking words right out of a person's mouth. This is exactly how Helene and I feel. We have, frankly, been miserable away from here, including Eve. Our place is here for so many reasons. This is just one more compelling justification. We should all be here for ourselves and to give back to the mothers what they have given us all of our lives. The farm and shelter are additional reasons for us all to be together as a family. Some families have no choice and cannot be together. We can be together, and all of our lives will be richer for it."

"Let's all do it!" The echo in the heart reverberated throughout the room.

FAMILY

The essence of family defies an adequate description,
  The powerful bond of unity reaching every moment;
It adds a special meaning to each situation,
  Mutual support softens any undue disappointment.

After all, family is a feeling, a pervasive security,
  A shield from danger and offense;
Its presence provides a cushion for futility,
  And imbues reality in the face of pretense.

The love of and within a family is a precious gift,
  It is irreplaceable and a constant positive;
It is the needed anchor when set adrift,
  The valuable example for each member to live.

Family is the magical connection of each together or apart,
It is the special love that is the echo in the heart.

Daniel Hill Zafren